Open the Green Door to a world of mystery pleasure ... literate entertainment for fans of the best writers at their very best ... Rex Stout, Manning Coles, Patricia Wentworth and many others. A complete list of Green Door mysteries will be found on the next page.

GIDEON AND MARRIC

Commander George Gideon of Scotland Yard's C.I.D. is one of the most fascinating—and most "human"—detectives of recent years. Readers have followed him—his exciting work, his problems with his staff and with his family—through several best-selling books. In 1962, a Gideon novel—GIDEON'S FIRE—won the coveted "Edgar" award of the Mystery Writers of America as the Best Mystery of the Year.

Gideon's creator, J. J. Marric, is in reality the incredibly prolific John Creasey—with over 300 novels, sales of more than two million copies, eight pseudonyms, and over a quarter-century of writing experience to his credit.

And with all this quantity goes work of the highest quality. As Anthony Boucher, writing in The New York Times Book Review, points out: "His best work . . . must be ranked among the best crime fiction of today. No one in any country has handled the novel of straightforward police routine more effectively than Creasey in the books signed 'J. J. Marric.' "

GREEN DOOR MYSTERIES

A Green Door Mystery

GIDEON'S WEEK

(Previously published as SEVEN DAYS TO DEATH)

J. J. MARRIC

▲

PYRAMID BOOKS • NEW YORK

GIDEON'S WEEK

(Previously published as *Seven Days to Death*)

A PYRAMID BOOK—
published by arrangement with
Harper & Brothers

PRINTING HISTORY—Harper & Brothers edition published 1956
Pyramid edition published March 1958
Second printing, December 1963

PYRAMID BOOKS are published by Pyramid Publications, Inc.,
444 Madison Avenue, New York 22, New York, U.S.A.

1 . Report for Gideon

As George Gideon of the Criminal Investigation Department drove from his home to Scotland Yard that Monday morning, a report was being prepared for him. He knew that it would be ready by the time he reached his office, and could imagine the antics of Lemaitre and the others helping to prepare it. He remembered performing similar antics, long before he had become Commander Gideon. This newly-created title irked him a little; in many ways he preferred the old "Chief Superintendent." Still, "Commander" had advantages, and really meant what it said. Gideon, above everything else a human being, enjoyed the warm glow which springs from reaching the top of the tree.

He had a fairly good idea of what would be in the report, too, although no one had telephoned him since he had left the Yard late on Friday evening. In general terms, he would receive a summary of the crimes committed in the Greater London area during the week end, as well as a résumé of what had happened during the previous week; the report would name all the suspects who had been charged and were now on remand; and would also give the names of suspects against whom there was not enough evidence for an arrest. If the Yard had only to stretch out a hand and pick up those offenders who were known to have committed a crime, life would be comparatively easy. Gideon's first mentor in the Criminal Investigation Department had been fond of saying that the burden of proof was the heaviest burden the Yard had to carry. Trite but true.

It was a mild spring morning, welcome after several bitter weeks and snowfalls which had twice dislocated London traffic and had covered most of the British Isles. As a policeman, Gideon liked cold weather. Those members of his erring flock who worked under cover of darkness—and that was most of them—disliked cold winds, cold hands, shivery corners and slippery roads. They had to be quick and they had to be quiet, so it wasn't surprising that there was less crime during exceptionally cold spells. The one which had just passed had been one of the coldest and quietest.

Among the things which made Gideon different from most policemen, and probably the greatest single factor in his early promotion—for to be Commander of the C.I.D. at the age of forty-nine was quite remarkable—was the way he looked upon simple facts such as the effect of wintry weather on those crooks who worked by night. To most police, the cold spell simply meant that the bad men wouldn't get around so much. So life would be quieter, the magistrates' courts less busy, the telephone less urgent and the insurance companies less active. Gideon saw beyond all this. He saw hungry crooks, their patient wives, their children going to school so close to the edge of hunger that it might affect them for most of their lives. Gideon wasn't simply being humanitarian when he recognized the fact that a crook could be as fond of his wife and children as any copper, and be just as anxious to keep them well fed.

With so many burglars nearly desperate to earn money, as soon as the weather broke, there was likely to be a big crop of crimes. The Divisions, especially the uniformed men, might be off their guard because of the recent lull. That was a thing to prevent.

As Gideon drove round Parliament Square and was held up by a traffic policeman first at the end of Parliament Street and then at the approach to the Embankment, the duty policeman recognized and saluted him. He drove slowly along the Embankment, hardly aware of the Thames stretching out so far ahead, dull and flat in the pale morning mist. Nearing the Yard, he saw a Squad car swing out of the wide gateway, turn away from him, and go hurtling toward Blackfriars and the City. Something was up, or a Squad car wouldn't be going at such speed. He watched the driver weaving in and out of traffic with the effortless control which marked him as better than average, even for the Flying Squad.

Then Gideon turned into the Yard.

One of the advantages of his new rank was the fact that parking space was always left for him. True, his name wasn't on it, but neither was the Assistant Commissioner's C.I.D. on his, or the Commissioner's for that matter. All the same, no one would pirate their place or Gideon's.

He got out and wound up the windows. The car, a black Wolseley, had a few surface scratches, but for a year-old model it had been kept very well. He was beginning to feel affection for it, as for a spirited horse. He turned toward the steps which led into the C.I.D. building, well aware that he was being watched not only by all the plain clothes and uniformed men in sight, some coming and some going, but also by people at the windows and almost certainly by a sergeant who was now nipping along to his office and telling Chief Inspector Lemaitre that the Boss was on the way.

What Gideon did not know was that those who had no need to be wary of him were also aware, by a kind of telepathy, that he was here. And of course he didn't really know what he looked like. He realized that he was big; but so were many men at the yard. It did not occur to him that none of these others had quite his massive hugeness, or his great breadth of shoulder. He was six feet two, and his fondness for the comfort of loose-fitting clothes made him look even bigger than he was. He walked casually, as if out for a stroll, and with a steady rhythm which, given the right circumstances, held a kind of menace. Walking, Gideon looked as if he knew exactly where he was going, when and how he wanted to get there, and that nothing and nobody would be able to put him off his course.

Lemaitre would now be crossing the t's and dotting the i's of the report, he mused, smiling dryly to himself. So the news flashed round the Yard that Gideon was in a sunny mood.

He reached the top of the steps, and the duty sergeant smiled a familiar welcome, while younger men were more formal. At the lift, with its one-armed operator, he found another man waiting to go up, a comparative youngster in plain clothes. This man was fresh-faced, had bright blue eyes, and was dressed in a carefully pressed navy blue suit which looked embarrassingly new. He stiffened when Gideon got in, as if he would readily press himself into the side of the lift.

"Hallo, Joe," Gideon greeted the liftman.

"Bit milder, isn't it?" the liftman said with the casualness of a man who had been taking senior officials up and down for twenty-odd years.

"Morning, sir," the fresh-complexioned young man said, and turned a brighter red.

"Morning," responded Gideon, and tipped his trilby hat to the back of his head; he felt warm. "You're Abbott, aren't you?"

"That's right, sir!" The man was delighted, and that meant one good thing; he was not likely to get blasé or too cocksure—at least, not until he was past the dangerous formative days for a detective officer at the Yard. Looked a nice lad. Twenty-six or seven, Gideon hazarded. He'd been blooded when on the beat in a running battle with two thieves and a stolen car, had come through with a black eye, a sprained ankle and a week's sick-leave, and the thieves were still inside. Gideon, knowing about this as he acquired knowledge about everyone at the Yard, couldn't decide whether or not to mention it. Better not risk giving Abbott a swelled head. It would be wiser to send him off with a different kind of satisfaction.

"Likely to have a burst of bad-man trouble the next few days, if the weather holds," Gideon said.

"Are we, sir?"

Gideon thought: As honest as they come. Keep that way. "Usually do as soon as we thaw out a bit," he went on, and actually found himself wondering whether, in twenty-five years' time, this same Abbott would remember it as an axiom, as he, Gideon, had remembered the one about the burden of proof.

The lift stopped, Abbott kept back, Gideon nodded and went out. Here he was just round the corner from the office which he shared with Chief Inspector Lemaitre. He wasn't surprised to see the door open an inch; that would give Lemaitre and anyone with him the split second of warning they imagined they needed. He wondered if Lemaitre had thought of sending a note round to the Divisions, saying that they could expect more trouble than they'd been having lately. Probably not.

He pushed open the door.

Lemaitre, tall, thinnish and lanky, was standing up by the telephone, coat off, collar undone, red tie hanging down, thin dark hair smoothed flat, a film of sweat on his forehead. Heat struck Gideon as he went in, although all four office windows, overlooking the Embankment and the Thames, were open as wide as they could be.

"Okay," Lemaitre said, and put the receiver down. "Cor," he said, "what a morning! First time we've had the central heating working properly this year, I should think. Trust those ruddy maintenance men to choose the first warm morning. I'd—"

Gideon shut the door.

"Morning, Lem," he said.

Lemaitre grinned.

"Morning, George. Had a nice week end?"

"Bit of all right," said Gideon, "didn't do a damned thing and it toned me up nicely for the week. How about you?" He was already loosening his collar; it was really steaming hot and unpleasant. He glanced at the big radiator; Lemaitre had turned the heat off, so the room should soon cool down.

"So so," said Lemaitre; "it's a funny thing that whenever you have a week end off, all the nuisance jobs come up, or else the things you know most about. They're all in the report. Pretty slack, generally."

"Yes." Gideon sat down behind his big desk, where the report was waiting, mostly typewritten but with the last-minute additions in Lemaitre's almost copperplate handwriting. "What's on this morning? Saw a Squad car go out."

"Safe been blown at Kelly's Bank, Fleet Street," said Lemaitre. "I've told Dooley to get ready to go over there, and King-Hadden's sending over right away. No night watchman, so the job might have been done any time over the week end, cold as a stone now. Still, you never know." There was Lemaitre, doing the thing which would always keep him down to C.I.'s rank—jumping to conclusions. He couldn't help it, and nothing would now be able to stop him. His manner and his tone told the story clearly: he didn't expect to get much in the way of results.

"Who's the Squad car driver, d'you know?"

"Soon find out," said Lemaitre, and plucked at the telephone as Gideon sat down, coat already off, and perspiration beginning to break out on his forehead. "Only thing of real interest cropped up since Friday is that they've got that kid for the Primrose Girl job."

Gideon looked up quickly. "Sure?"

"Cast-iron. Fingerprints, footprints, his knife, known to have been with her on Thursday afternoon, jealous because she threw him over. Named Rose. Funny, isn't it?"

"What's funny?" asked Gideon almost sharply, but Lemaitre had switched from him to the telephone. Gideon studied his assistant almost as if he were looking at someone he didn't know well, but his tension eased while Lemaitre talked.

"That you, Freddy? . . . No, rest easy, the Boss is in and wants to know who was driving our car on the Kelly's Bank job. . . . Oh, Sammy Brown . . . dunno, hold on a minute." Lemaitre lowered the receiver but asked so that both the Squad chief and Gideon could hear. "Anything wrong, he wants to know."

"He's a good driver, don't waste him on the easy jobs," Gideon said. "I'll have a word with Freddy a bit later on."

He glanced through the nine pages of the typewritten report, and near the end reached the item about the arrest and charging of one, William Sydney Rose, for the murder of Winifred Ethel Norton, known as the Primrose Girl because she had died with a little bunch of primroses clutched in her left hand. On Friday morning, it had been the newspaper story of the week, perhaps of the month.

There wasn't much here. Routine checking had led them to William Sydney Rose because he was known as a friend of the girl's. This was mainly a Divisional job, although a Yard man had been present at the time of the arrest.

"What's funny about it?" Gideon asked.

"Eh? I didn't know anything was—oh, Rose?" Lemaitre grinned. "You slipping, George? The Primrose Girl murdered by a man named Rose, see. Rose."

Gideon looked down at the report.

"Hm. They haven't picked up anyone for the Battersea hit-and-run job, have they?"

"No," said Lemaitre.

He gathered from Gideon's manner that this wasn't likely to be a talking session, after all, and he didn't greatly mind. He sat down, lit a cigarette with a lighter which wouldn't work properly, and glanced at the dark, ugly nicotine stain on his fingers. Then he started to work on two or three routine reports that would have to be vetted by Gideon before they were sent to the Assistant Commissioner.

Between nine and ten in the morning the telephone was usually quiet—well, quieter than at other times. It didn't ring for fifteen minutes. In that time Gideon had read the report through quickly and marked certain paragraphs for a more careful reading. There wasn't a great deal. Seven burglaries Saturday night, four last night.

Two fires, one with arson suspected. The usual crop of drunk and disorderlies on Saturday, the usual week-end harvest of West End streetwalkers, a bottle-and-broken-glass fight outside a Stepney public house with both protagonists in hospital but neither on the danger list. Expected arrest connected with some currency frauds, a warning from Switzerland about a man on his way by air, believed to have five hundred watches hidden in his luggage. Nothing really sensational. Nothing to presage an abnormal week, except the mild weather. Nothing to get under Gideon's skin except the Primrose Girl. You could be as tough as you liked, but there were weak spots. He had three daughters and three sons; his second daughter had been out picking primroses in a sheltered spot in Surrey on Thursday afternoon. The Primrose Girl had been out picking primroses in a sheltered spot in Kent the same afternoon; and while she had been there, she had been savagely attacked, with eleven knife wounds in the chest. Gideon had seen photographs but not the body. He had also seen the photograph of the girl's left hand, tight about some withered primroses.

The telephone broke the quiet.

A telephone call to Gideon could be the prelude to anything from a high-powered murder investigation to a summons from the Assistant Commissioner for Crime to go and see him. It could be some routine question or piece of information. It could be from a squealer with information to sell. It could be his tailor, to tell him that his new suit was ready for fitting; it would even be one of his elder children or his wife, although they seldom troubled him at the office. The essential thing, as Gideon knew, was that when he picked up the telephone he should have a completely open mind; and that he shouldn't be preoccupied. One thing at a time was always safest.

He didn't get any sense of impending disaster.

He didn't flicker an eyelid when the operator said, "It's Mr. Ripley, of Manchester, sir."

Ripley was his opposite number with the Manchester City C.I.D.

"Put him through."

Lemaitre glanced up, and Gideon mouthed, "Manchester."

"Could be that slush job; they picked up about sixty-five-one-pounders on Friday," Lemaitre said at once.

Gideon nodded, but he didn't share the opinion. Ripley

of Manchester wouldn't telephone him about a job that was already known at the Yard. He knew Ripley too well to think that. They had met first during their early days in the Force; and as far as Gideon had close friends, Ripley was one.

There were the usual noises on the line, and Gideon waited patiently for Ripley's voice, with those broad a's and something like t' for "the." Only one thing was certain: Ripley would not ring him on long distance unless he was prodded by a sense of real urgency.

Then a voice that was not Ripley's came on the line.

"Sorry, Commander, but the Superintendent's been called away in a hurry. He'll ring you as soon as he can."

"That suits me," said Gideon patiently, "but what's it all about?"

The other said, "Mass escape from Millways jail, it's keeping us well on the hop up here. Mr. Ripley wanted you to have word quickly. I'll ring you again, sir."

The Manchester man rang off before Gideon spoke.

2 . The Escape

Gideon put down the receiver slowly, telling Lemaitre what the trouble was, as he did so. Lemaitre got up, fumbled for a cigarette from a packet, and lit it as he was halfway across the office. His eyes were screwed up, and his lips pursed. "Mass escape?" he asked; and when Gideon nodded but didn't speak, he stopped in front of Gideon's desk and then perched on a corner. "I'll bet that means Benson's out."

Gideon brought out his dark cherrywood pipe, with the big bowl that was rough on the outside, something to fiddle with at the moment, and not to smoke.

"Lem, why don't you give it a rest? There are over a thousand prisoners at Millways, and I don't suppose more than half a dozen have got away. There isn't any reason to think that Benson's one of them."

Lemaitre had the sense not to argue.

"What beats me," Gideon went on, "is how they've managed an escape up there this week end. All Lancashire had another blizzard Saturday; I was told the place was snowed up, especially out near Millways. Funny business."

"I could ring Manchester, and—"

"Tell you what we'd better do," said Gideon; "get the

rest of the work as clear as we can, in case we have to spend time on this job. Not that anyone who escaped from Millways can have got as far south as this. Now, let's get a move on."

"Okay, George," said Lemaitre, just managing to keep the note of resignation out of his voice. "What goes?"

"First, put a flash out to all Squad and patrol cars to keep a specially keen watch today, tell them that now it's warmer we might find some of the boys getting busy. That will spread out from the patrol cars to the Divisions. Then get me the fullest report you can from the Division on the Primrose Girl job. Find out if Birdy's better this morning and carrying on at the Old Bailey; heck of a mess when a judge falls ill and a trial has to be interrupted. Then . . ."

Instructions, suggestions and questions streamed from Gideon as water from a tap. Soon he was sending for sergeants, for Detective-Inspectors and Chief Inspectors to give brief reports on jobs they were doing. He kept his voice pitched low, and did not give the impression that he paid much attention to what was being said, but every man who entered the office knew better than that. In some ways they knew even better than Gideon himself, because they could watch from the outside. In his way he was a fascinating object lesson. He absorbed information so accurately that he seemed to be almost as familiar with each job as the men who were working on it; a kind of C.I.D. Memory Man. If he didn't get a point clearly, he worried it. And he put out suggestions about how to handle a job, sometimes carefully wrapped up, occasionally twisted so that they seemed to emanate from the man he was talking to. It was a form of briefing which Gideon himself had introduced, and had become almost part of the tradition at the Yard. Sometimes it lasted all morning; today it was over in an hour.

Three times senior officers had asked if he knew what had happened at Millways; the rumor was already spreading, and had probably been started by the telephone operator, unless there was a teleprint message in. He checked; he didn't want operators talking too freely. There had been a teleprint, received a little while after he had spoken to the man from Manchester, but it gave only one additional piece of information.

Nine men had escaped. Five were named, but the man Benson wasn't among them. Didn't Millways *know* who'd gone, yet? They'd alert the local police the moment they knew about a break, of course, and nine would take a lot of checking.

"Why don't you call Ripley?" asked Lemaitre.

"He'll ring when he's ready." Gideon was still smoothing his pipe. It was much cooler in the office, but outside the mist was giving way to sunshine; the Thames could look good. Most mornings he would have gone for a stroll round London's Square Mile—his own particular beat, the one he'd walked for years before being planted on the desk—but the hope of an early call from Ripley stopped him.

Lemaitre went out of the office; there wasn't much doubt that he was trying to find out all he could about the Millways break, but Gideon didn't let himself think too much about it and hardly at all about Benson.

If Benson had escaped . . .

He was getting as bad as Lemaitre. As a matter of fact, this morning he was feeling sour toward Lem, although he couldn't really say why. His good mood hadn't developed, and for some reason he was on edge. That Primrose Girl job was under his skin, of course, and he knew that was a bad thing.

Then Ripley came through.

"That you, George?"

"What's the matter up there, Jim, everyone got frostbite?"

"When I've finished telling you what I think of this job at Millways, you'll have frostbite," growled Ripley. "As a matter of fact, George, it was a right smart piece of work; we have to give them that. They took advantage of the snow; in all about a hundred prisoners were involved in it, and nine got outside the prison walls. We've picked up two already. They built a kind of staircase in hard-packed snow, which had frozen hard, and went over the wall. Must have paid a screw to keep his back turned, but —well, that's not my worry now, that's the Governor's, and I wouldn't like to be in the Chief Warder's shoes this morning. Thing is, George, Benson's one of the seven who are still free."

Gideon said slowly: "Oh, is he?"

"When it's all come out, we'll probably find that Benson was behind the job," Ripley said. "There's just one good thing about it: he'll be afraid to show himself even if he does get out of the Manchester district, and there's no certainty that he'll do that yet. But I wanted to tell you in person, you know Benson and his boys better than anyone living, that's why I rang earlier, but the Chief Constable wouldn't wait. Anyway, there it is, George."

"Thanks," said Gideon.

"I know," said Ripley, in reply to unspoken comment, "they ought to have strung him up but they didn't. And I'm not so sure that a man who's been as near the gallows as Benson will give a damn about risking a life sentence. He's been at Millways for three years; it may have tamed him."

Gideon said dryly, "it looks as if it has, doesn't it? Who else got away? Anyone in the same mob?"

"Yes. Jingo Smith and Wally Alderman. The others are all solo workers. The list's on the teleprinter by now. Five Londoners, just to cheer you up. George, I'm not going to waste your time or mine, I know you'll do everything that needs doing. Let's hear from you one of these days."

"Okay, Jim," Gideon said. "Thanks for ringing."

He rang off, very slowly and thoughtfully.

He drew a pad toward him and made a note of several different people whom he wanted to talk to about the jail break, and steps he wanted them to take. But he didn't put a call in yet. In the brief and blessed quiet, he was able to think without feeling that he was being pushed—a condition which wouldn't last long. The escape of any prisoner meant high pressure until the man was found or else the hue and cry had died down, and Benson—well, this would mean newspaper headlines every day until Benson was captured. It would put fear into the hearts of several people, too. It would mean giving special protection to at least two people, including Benson's wife. All this was a long story, and Gideon, in a way, had grown up with it. The one overriding factor was simply this:

Benson was a killer. He should have been hanged. He was known to have killed at least two people over a period of eleven years, but the "burden of proof" had been too heavy. Finally, the police had got him on an attempted murder charge, but the victim hadn't died. It was hardly true to say that he lived, either; he was a mental and physical wreck and would have been better off dead. But the law didn't allow a man to be charged with murder because he had condemned another to a living death. Benson had been given fifteen years' penal servitude; he'd served three.

The telephone bell rang.

Gordon lifted the receiver. "Gideon."

"George." This was the Assistant Commissioner, crisply. "Can you spare me a minute?" He could have said simply, "Come and see me," but it wasn't his way.

"Yes, I'll come," Gideon said. "Right away." He pressed a bell and stood up; tightened his tie, shrugged himself into his coat, and smoothed down his thick, iron-gray hair. By that time he'd reached the door, and it was opened by a middle-aged, graying sergeant named Jefferson. "Jeff, stay here until Mr. Lemaitre or I get back, will you? I'll be with the A.C." Gideon nodded and went out walking in that characteristic way, not hurrying, and giving the impression that if anything should get in his path he would push it aside.

He heard the hurried footsteps of a man who couldn't move fast enough, and smothered a grin. This was Lemaitre, who came swinging round a corner, eyes very bright. He almost skidded to a standstill.

"It was Benson!" he blurted.

"Lem, there are times when you've got second sight," said Gideon. "Jefferson's in the office, I'm going to see the old man. You nip down to Records and get Benson's file, will you—and the files of Benson's pals, Wally Alderman and Jingo Smith."

"They out, too?"

"Yes. Get the names of the others, have the files out, then call the five people I've jotted down on my note pad, and tell them to keep their eyes open. If we don't pick up Benson soon, we might run into a lot of trouble."

"It had to break sooner or later," Lemaitre said. "Been too quiet for a long time. Okay. Like a cushion for your pants?"

The A.C.'s office was on the same floor as Gideon's, overlooking almost an identical scene. It was larger, it had only one desk, and there was a communicating door to his secretary's and personal assistant's office. Tall, lean, tough-looking, the A.C. was dressed in a suit of light gray tweed tailored to fit so perfectly that it looked almost too small. He had thin, crimpy hair, parted in the middle with a wide, pale parting.

"Hallo, George, come and sit down. Have a good week end?"

"Fine, thanks."

"About the first you've had in six weeks, but at least you had some sun yesterday. Sit down." Gideon lowered himself into a wooden armchair. "What have you done about the Millways business? Or haven't you had a chance, yet?"

Gideon smiled in the way he did only when he was with someone he liked.

"Not much," he said, "Lemaitre's on the job now. I'm warning the Divisions where the London men came from to watch their homes. I'm having two of our chaps go round to Mrs. Benson's place to keep an eye on her, better not leave that to the Divisions; and I'm putting out a general call, London and Home Counties as from now, to keep their eyes open. Then I'm getting photographs printed of all the men for the *Police Gazette* and for the police stations. If we pick Benson up in a few hours, we'll have wasted a little money and a lot of time. If we don't, then we'll be off to a good start."

"Every now and again, when I get to thinking seriously, I tell myself that I ought to spend more time in the garden; while you're here, this place works better without me." The A.C. wasn't smiling. "Benson was a man I didn't have much to do with, I've only read and heard about him. This is the first time I've ever believed that he was as bad as the report said. You've convinced me."

"No report is bad enough," Gideon told him flatly; "but when you work it out, he hasn't much chance of getting far, has he? The country's snowbound north of a line from the Severn to the Wash. Manchester's picked up two of the escapers already, and there's a sound chance they'll all be in their cells again before the night's out. With a bit of luck, it will all die down."

"All right, let's look on the bright side," agreed the A.C. "But I didn't really want to talk about that—I'd hardly got round to it. His eyes smiled. "This man Rose and the Primrose Girl murder—have you seen the Divisional report?"

"No, just a précis."

"It looks cut and dried," said the A.C., "but Smedd over at H5 has put in reports that make me think." He passed over some papers, including a photograph of William Rose; and a note said that Rose was twenty years old. "Usually, when a kid is caught and held on a job like this and told what the buildup is, he confesses," the A.C. observed. "He retracts afterward, of course, under the influence of a lawyer who tells him he must do better than that, because lies might save him. But this boy just insists that he didn't do it. Smedd says he keeps quite calm—not at all like most youngsters. Comes from a family with a good background; his father died only three months ago. The mother's distraught. He's got two sisters—one older, one younger than he is." The A.C. had a habit of dispensing information like this in a casual, off-hand way, almost as if he felt guilty at having it. "Smedd seems absolutely sure of himself, but I'd like to see young Rose. Will you ring Smedd when you can fit it in? He'd bring Rose here —unless you're going over that way."

"Could do, a bit later," said Gideon. "I'll have a look at it. That the lot?

"Not quite." The A.C. grimaced. "The Public Prosecutor's wishing a new boy onto us, and he's coming over to have a talk about the case against Edmundsun. It's the new chap's first embezzlement prosecution; and if you ask me, he'll want wet-nursing. Who would you let him talk to? I don't mean Gideon!"

Gideon said thanks, as if he really meant it. Then,

"Cummings," he said, "unless the new boy's too conscious of his position as a prosecutor for the Crown, and must have a C.I."

"He'll have what I give him."

"Cummings knows that job inside out. He's a bit young, but if he sees this through and we put Edmundsun inside, I'd move him up. Not that it'll be easy, Edmundsun's pretty fly. That the lot?"

"Yes. In a hurry?"

"It wouldn't surprise me if things keep us on the go all day," said Gideon. "There's enough on my plate until middle afternoon already."

He went out, without hurrying. He had long passed the time when he paused to reflect that he and the Yard were lucky with the A.C., and yet a conference, as this one, always did him good. He was completely over his sour mood, too. He'd recovered from the sharp blow of the news from Manchester and was moving into a different frame of mind, the attacking one, in which he could really spread himself. And he'd find a chance to slip out for an hour. Much better to see the Rose boy at Divisional H.Q. than it would be here; Scotland Yard had a peculiar effect on many people, especially people on a charge but new to police methods.

Gideon went into his office.

Lemaitre was saying, "Half a mo, here he is." He lowered the receiver and pressed it against his chest as he looked up at Gideon. "Girl downstairs in the hall asking for you, George; says it's important. Won't give her name, but says she's a friend of your Pru, too."

Gideon was almost knocked back on his heels in surprise.

"Friend of Pru's, wanting me?"

"That's the size of it."

Gideon said, "Well, all right, I'll go and see what she wants. You haven't finished those calls yet, have you?"

"No one's called me lightning yet," said Lemaitre.

Gideon went out and made his way in the opposite direction, toward the lift. It wasn't often that he was completely at a loss, but he was now. Prudence, his eldest daughter, had a lot of friends in a world that Gideon didn't even begin to know: the musical world. She played the violin well enough to win a place in the Home Counties Philharmonic Orchestra, and he understood that at nineteen that was remarkable. She could hardly have sent this friend to see him, or she would have said so; at least she'd have rung him up and warned him.

The unexpected was always the thing to tackle first.

Gideon had a word with Joe, at the lift, and two C.I.'s, the only topic being the Millways break. Then he reached the hall.

The girl waiting there was about Pru's age, he thought, rather fresh and pretty, with a very smooth complexion, blue eyes and not much make-up. She looked rather familiar. As he went toward her, Gideon thought that if ever he had seen trouble, it was in this girl's eyes. She was nervous, too, although obviously trying hard to conceal it. She recognized Gideon on sight, took a short step toward him and then hesitated, as if she didn't know what to say. To try to put her at her ease, he smiled as he might have at Prudence.

Then he realized why she looked familiar.

She was like William Rose, who had been arrested for the Primrose Girl's murder, like him as a sister might be.

3 . Alibi for Rose?

There was a hard streak in Gideon; had there not been, he would never have reached his position. He dealt in facts and had learned to repress any emotion which might entice him to look on facts from the wrong angle. His master was the Law; and he not only served it but knew that if he or anyone else deviated from it he was likely to store up serious trouble. So over the years he had cultivated the hard streak; and there were some who saw this but did not see the other side of his nature, the sentimental side.

This revealed itself particularly where young people were involved. It wasn't surprising, seeing that he had his own brood of half a dozen, but the real explanation lay in the past. There had been a seventh child, a boy who had died while Gideon had been out on a job, although his wife had beseeched him not to go. The tangled emotions, the self-blame, the remorse, the emotional upheaval within Kate, his wife, for long afterward, had made a deep mark on Gideon; but at least he knew that he was most vulnerable whenever the young were the trouble. That was why from the beginning he had been so anxious to know about the Primrose Girl and her murder—and the boy under arrest. Now, he did not doubt that he was face to face with the boy's sister.

She was nervous of him, almost frightened.

He supposed she was twenty-one, certainly not much more. Her brown hair was a feathery kind of cluster, her eyes were honey-colored. She had on only a trace of lipstick, and her lips were set tightly, as if she was afraid that if she opened her mouth the muscles would take control and she would burst out crying.

Gideon knew that the sergeant and a constable on duty were watching her as intently as he.

There might be a lot of doubt about what to do later, but for the moment he had just to set this girl at ease and smooth out that tension. So he hardly paused as he moved toward her, but maintained his pleasant smile and offered her his hand. With two or three words, too, he did the thing which mattered more perhaps than anything: he gave her a sense of his omniscience.

20

"Hallo, Miss Rose," he said. "I didn't know you were a friend of Pru's, so many things one's daughter doesn't tell one about." Her hand was cold, but the quick nervous pressure told him that he was already making an impression. "I didn't keep you waiting, I hope."

She managed to say: "No, I—no." She bit her lips, and he saw that tears were stinging her eyes. She couldn't find words, now that she was here; all her strength had gone, on finding the courage to come and ask for him.

He took her arm, much as he would Pru's.

"We can go along here and sit down," he said; and as he led her toward a small waiting room just along the passage, he added to the sergeant, "How about some tea, Matt?"

"Right away, sir."

"Say ten minutes," Gideon said.

The room was a small one, with a window overlooking the barracks-like square, where the Squad and other cars were parked. The window was barred, because occasionally they had a tough customer in here. It had been freshly painted, the walls were a shiny green below and yellow above, there were two armchairs, some upright chairs, a table, ash tray, and—the inevitable wall decoration at the Yard—photographs of sporting giants or teams of the past.

The girl probably noticed nothing of this.

The touch of Gideon's big hand and the minute's walk to this room had helped her. She didn't fight so hard to keep back tears, dabbed at her eyes with a handkerchief, and then blew her nose. Was she a smoker? Gideon took out a fat cigarette case, which he carried only to be sociable.

"No—no, I don't smoke," she said, looking at him intently, and speaking huskily but without a quiver in her voice. "How—how did you know who I was? I didn't tell anyone."

"You're very like your brother," said Gideon, "and I remembered your name, from the A.C.'s report: Mary."

That remark stung her, and she had to turn away again, but only for a moment.

"Yes, I am," she said stiffly. "He—he *didn't* kill Winifred."

"Didn't he?"

"No."

"Positive?"

"He couldn't have," William Rose's sister said.

She said it in such a way that Gideon felt a current of warning; this wasn't going to be just the sentimental, emotional appeal which might have been expected. She was a courageous little customer—hadn't she proved it, by getting him to come and see her by using Pru's name?

"If you're sure he couldn't have, can you help us to prove it?" Gideon asked, watching her very closely. She was no longer looking away from him; her eyes were wide open and steady, shining with a kind of defiance. He went on in the same quiet and convincing voice. "The last thing we want to do is to hold an innocent man and make him go through this kind of ordeal."

"That's what you say."

"It's what I mean."

"Well, the men who arrested Will didn't behave like that; they took it for granted that he was guilty from the beginning," the girl said hotly. "I was there when they came to see him, and then took him away. The way they talked to me was just the same. They even told me not to waste any time in lying to try to save him!"

Gideon thought: Oh, did they? but he wasn't wholly surprised. The Superintendent at H5 was coasting along toward retirement, and the Division wasn't running as smoothly as anyone outside it would have liked—or many inside it, for that matter. And, as often happened when there was any kind of weakness, two or three of the senior men had become a bit too big for their boots, showing a kind of truculence, a hardness, almost a callousness which didn't do anyone any good. You might talk to an old lag as the police had obviously talked to young Rose, but not to a boy without a record, who was one of a closely knit family, who . . .

"Perhaps they felt quite sure that he did kill this girl," Gideon said quietly.

"But he couldn't have!"

"Why not?"

"I was with him at the time he was supposed to have been with her," said Mary Rose.

"Were you?" asked Gideon, slowly.

He didn't believe her; and now he understood why the H5 men had been impatient. If she had attempted to give her brother an alibi, and they had reason to think that she was lying—well, they'd soon get annoyed. Policemen shouldn't, but they did. He could applaud the girl's effort and her spirit and at the same time feel desperately sorry for her, because she wouldn't have a chance to fool him or anyone else. She was as transparent as a mother trying to save the life of her child.

"Yes, I was," the girl said, more tensely. "We went to the pictures together."

It was building up to form. She claimed that they'd been to the cinema at a time when the house was crowded, throngs waiting to go in, no one able to pick out two youngsters from the hundreds of couples who had been moving to and fro. The pattern of this kind of alibi was so clear that Gideon—and the H5 men—could almost put Mary's words into her mouth.

Gideon didn't intend to.

"Mary," he said, and the use of her Christian name startled her again, "have you made an official statement about this to the police?"

"No. No, I . . ."

"Well, you'll have to," Gideon said briskly. "I'll arrange for someone to come and take the statement down, and then you can come back this afternoon, read it, and sign it. I don't want to miss the slightest clue, the slightest piece of evidence; but I can't do all these things personally, you know, and I haven't been dealing with the case myself."

"If only you would!" she cried.

The truth about Mary Rose, Gideon realized as he studied her, was that she was a young woman, not just a girl. Girls didn't have a figure like that: she was almost fully mature. She had the freshness which no man could fail to approve, and a simplicity which carried her to the point of naïveté. In an idle moment he would run his gaze up and down her figure, from her nice legs to her high bosom, and get that rather warm feeling that the sight of someone so young and desirable always gave. He didn't think she knew that her "If only you would!" might have come from the most disingenuous woman of the world; she probably didn't know just how much she seemed to be intent on flattering him.

"Well, the case is under my authority and there's no reason why I shouldn't look into it," he said practically, "but I've got to do what every other detective has to do: look at the evidence. That's the thing that matters, you know—evidence. Like your statement. When you've signed it, we shall have it as evidence, and if this case comes before the judge and jury, then you'll have to stand up in court and swear, on oath, that the statement was true in every detail." This was where she should begin to wilt, of course, but she didn't. "Then, if the jury believes you—well, that would be that. The verdict might depend on whether there is any contradictory evidence: if someone else saw your brother in a different place about the time . . ."

"They couldn't have, he was with me," said Mary Rose, quietly.

For the first time Gideon began to wonder whether he could have been wrong, whether he was doing a Lemaitre by jumping to any kind of conclusion.

"And you'll make that statement and sign it?"

"Of course I will."

"Good," Gideon said, more briskly. "I'll bring a sergeant along; but before I do, tell me why you lied about being a friend of my daughter, will you?"

He looked very stern, then; as he might with Pru.

The girl flushed a little, not very much. "Well—well, it wasn't really a lie," she asserted. Under his gaze, she turned a deeper red, but stuck to her guns. "I do know Pru, slightly. We met at the Guildhall School of Music when I was studying the piano. She used to tell me—she used to tell us," Mary corrected, and now her face was almost scarlet, "that she was absolutely sure you wouldn't lie about a case. She—well, we used to ask her about you, because you were interesting. Everyone's fascinated by a real detective. We used to egg Pru on to talk about you, and—and in a way we—I seemed to know you."

Now Gideon had to hide a smile; she was laying it on with a trowel, yet obviously didn't realize it; and she had a case.

"I see," he said. "That explains it."

She went on very quickly: "And when this awful thing happened and the other police wouldn't listen to me, I remembered everything Pru had said and just had to come and see you. I didn't think you'd see me if you knew who I was, but a friend of Pru—well, I had to see you."

"You know, Mary," Gideon said prosaically, "anyone who has a good reason for wanting to see me or anyone else at Scotland Yard can always come. You don't need special influence. And whether your brother is guilty or not, we want to help you and your mother and . . ."

He broke off.

Tears had filled the girl's eyes again, and suddenly she

seemed more heavily burdened than at any time since they had come into this room. She couldn't meet his eyes. She just sat there, hands gripping the arms of her chair, head turned toward the barred window, lips so tight together that he knew she was trying to keep back an outburst of tears. She wasn't just a nice kid fighting for her brother; she was a young woman keyed up to a terrible pitch of emotional tension; her nerves were as taut as nerves could be, and something had twanged them. Gideon wasn't sorry that there was a tap at the door, and the constable came in with the tea and some biscuits.

"Put that down here," Gideon said to him, and then in a low-pitched voice: "Have a policewoman here in ten minutes, tell her to bring some aspirins." The policeman nodded, and Gideon turned round to the girl, then poured out a cup of tea, and went on: "Better have this while it's hot, Mary."

Now she looked at him, but made no attempt to take the tea.

"You don't believe me," she said drearily, "no one believes me, but it's true, it's absolutely true. We were at the pictures. Will had had a quarrel with Win and was ever so upset. He hadn't any money, and I—I treated him. But no one will believe me."

If she'd added, "And I'm so frightened," she would have told Gideon everything.

It was certainly time he went to see young William Rose.

The policewoman, who wasn't so much older than the girl, took over; she didn't need telling what to do. Gideon sent for a stenographer to take down the statement, and hovered between thinking that he was a fool to be half-persuaded, and that he was a hardhearted cynic not to take Mary Rose at her word. As he left the waiting room, he knew that it had been one of those interludes which would never be wholly forgotten. He'd bring this girl to mind at odd times when he was thinking of Pru, or talking to her. He'd learned a lot, too. Pru, sitting at the School of Music, talking to a group of students, cashing in on being the daughter of a Yard detective! Pru was the one of his children he would never have suspected of pride. But it wasn't all a matter of tolerant, rather smug amusement. There was this girl and her dread; Rose's mother and sister—and the dead girl. Remember, she had been stabbed eleven times with William Rose's knife. Remember, they'd quarreled. And remember there was another family, the Primrose Girl's family, with their grief.

That was the trouble; once you started seeing the sentimental side, it didn't stop. His job was to find the facts. The truth, the whole truth and nothing but the truth, so help him God.

He went soberly upstairs, and by the time he reached his office, he had decided to go straight over to see young Rose, unless something had cropped up while he'd been downstairs.

The only thing he was more anxious about was Benson's escape.

4 . Benson

Benson was with a man twelve years younger than himself, named Freddy Tisdale.

Their partnership had been decided upon at the time of the original plan for the prison break. It hadn't originated in Benson's mind, but in the agile mind of Jingo Smith, the ideas man for the gang which Benson had led for several years before they had run into trouble, Gideon, and the immutable forces of the law.

There had been an early winter fall of snow, about the middle of December, and Jingo Smith had seen what might happen if there should be another heavy snowfall and a high wind. In fact, he remembered from the previous year that some of the drifts in the prison yard had been so high that, when frozen hard, they made a sloping bank from the yard itself to the top of the wall. The warders, of course, were well aware of it; and at times when there were big snowdrifts, the watch was doubled and the drifts cleared quickly. But Jingo had talked about this to Benson and Wally Alderman, and slowly and patiently they had developed the plan.

It had meant using trusties, of course. It had also meant the connivance of a warder—not to help in the escape, but to give one or two of the trusties special privileges which had enabled the plans to be laid. The conditions required had been quite apparent: a heavy snowfall, a high wind, and a disturbance in one part of the prison to enable the escapers to win their chance. At first they had planned for six of them to break out. Two more had been added to

the list; and, at the last moment, a ninth man had discovered what they were planning and had strung along
with them.

If they hadn't let him come, he might have squealed.
Benson had no faith at all in honor among thieves.

The actual break-out had gone perfectly, conditions
being absolutely right. The disturbance had been a fire
which had broken out in the laundry, compelling the
warders to pay special attention to that part of the prison.
The escapers had been in the library, which was on the
first floor overlooking the prison yard. A file, smuggled in
from the shoemaker's shop, and a cobbler's hammer had
enabled them to break the iron bars and the toughened
glass. They'd got out, nipping across the six inches of snow
and up the slope as swift as antelopes. The librarian and
the two other warders with him had been overpowered
and trussed up; and no other prisoners had been in the
library at that time.

All had gone perfectly.

That was partly because Benson, having accepted the
idea, had worked it out.

That day, with Freddy Tisdale, he hid in a house not a
mile from the prison.

And he was ravenously hungry.

Benson wasn't a big man, just average. He did not seem
exceptionally strong, although he was. He looked hard.
He had sharp, chiseled features and pale blue eyes which
could look at a man squarely even though everything he
himself was saying was a lie. Hoping for the blizzard, he
had made most of the escapers avoid having haircuts, on
one pretext or another; only the last-minute man had a
prison crop. That was the kind of detail that Benson
excelled in, and was why he had been one of the most
successful criminals in England for nearly fifteen years.

He had overlooked only one detail, the one that had
sent him to jail. He had forgotten that his wife, having
learned to hate him, might give the police the evidence
they needed.

She had.

She was probably the only person in the world whom
Benson really hated.

There was no room for strong emotions in him, beyond
that. He had always approached every job, from burglary
to smash-and-grab, from beating-up to murder, quite cold-

bloodedly, being concerned only with what he might get out of it. The two men he had murdered had died simply because they could have named him and brought his career to an abrupt end. He hadn't hated them; he had had no feeling of any kind toward them.

He had never really loved, but his wife's beauty had bowled him over when they had met fifteen years ago. He had been proud of her for some time, until he had taken up with another girl who had no children to look after.

Benson's children, a boy and a girl, had meant little to him. It had never occurred to him that indirectly they had been responsible for his long prison sentence. Anxiety about the possible influence of a hardened criminal father upon the children had been the chief cause of his wife's "betrayal."

Now, Benson was on his way to see his wife.

He had arranged the pairing of the escape party, and had chosen Freddy Tisdale because Freddy had certain qualities which were the envy of almost everyone in the prison, and many hundreds outside. For one thing, he was double-jointed. For another, he was probably the finest locksmith in the country on the wrong side of the law; there was hardly a lock he couldn't force. And for the third, he looked such a kid. In a way, he was: just twenty-four. He was in prison because he and three other men had been caught red-handed in a fur salon, the locks of which Freddy had forced with insolent ease, and all four of them had beaten up a night watchman who had surprised them. They had been caught by police in a patrol car, while running away. The night watchman hadn't been badly hurt, and Freddy's share of the proceeds of the haul had been seven years.

Benson had realized that, behind the boyish, friendly face and the apparently resigned manner, there had lived in Freddy Tisdale the escape bug. You had it or you didn't have it. Nine men out of ten at Millways, the Moor, or any other prison, would no more dream of trying to escape than they would of spitting in the Governor's eyes. They knew that the prisoner was always caught and sent back, that he lost all his remission, made life much tougher for himself, and often faced a longer sentence because of new crimes committed while free. Perhaps one prisoner in ten would ignore these cold facts and long only for escape.

All nine of them had made it this time: a triumph.

Benson didn't know that two of them had already been

recaptured when, with Freddy Tisdale, he had reached the house where they were now hiding.

They had made a beeline for this spot because Benson knew that they wouldn't last long in the bitter cold and the snow unless they had some warm clothes, food, and rest. He'd picked the house out, with his dispassionate cunning, from the Houses to Let advertisements in the *Journal*, a local weekly newspaper which was available in the library at Millways, with certain items of news duly censored. Being a chatty, parochial weekly, there wasn't much blacked out, and Benson had made sure that, when studying the advertisement, he hadn't been noticed by the librarian or a warder.

There had been three houses to let furnished, and only one with an agent's name and address; this, Benson shrewdly suspected, meant that the house itself was empty at the time.

Another big advantage of having Freddy Tisdale with him was that Freddy knew the Millways district—every street, lane, and alley, almost every back yard. The police would watch Freddy's home, of course, and his friends; but to Benson Freddy's chief usefulness had been the ability to take him straight to 15 Nortoft Road, a semi-detached house in a street not far from the big canal. They had had to take a chance of some kind, and the chance they'd taken was coming here in daylight, with the risk of being seen by neighbors.

As far as they knew, they hadn't been seen. They had been here for several hours, no one had called, and they'd had plenty of luck. The main electricity was still on, and there were two electric heaters, which would not give off smoke or betray their presence in any way. They put the fires in a small room next to the kitchen, where there were armchairs, rugs and a radio which, tuned very low, was on all the time. This room had only one window; the curtain had been drawn when they arrived. They had spent some time blacking this out so that they could put on a light without being noticed.

Benson was quietly congratulating himself. In fact, there was only one thing wrong: he was hungry. In fact, he was so ravenous that it was a gnawing ache inside him. He even felt annoyed with Freddy, because Freddy didn't complain about the lack of food, just took it like a stoic.

The larder had been absolutely bare, without even an old packet of biscuits or any tins of food; nothing. Now,

four o'clock that afternoon, when it was still broad daylight outside, Benson felt sick with hunger, but knew that
neither of them dared break out until after dark. He had
spent a lot of time going over every detail of what had
happened, and didn't think that there was any risk of their
being discovered that night if they remained in the house.
They had been very thorough, and had even stopped near
the canal, tied some old sacks round their feet, and shuffled
along to the house; this way, there had been no footprints
in the snow.

Benson watched Freddy, who sat in an armchair on the
other side of the two fires, wearing a big coat which they
had found in a locked cupboard upstairs. Each of them
was warmly clad now, and the prison clothes were outside
in the scullery, drying. During the night, when no one
could see the smoke, these could be burned. They had also
found shoes, although these didn't fit very comfortably.
Freddy's were better, just a little loose on his small feet;
Benson's were too tight. That didn't matter now that he
could keep them unlaced, but he would have to lace them
up when he was outside.

Freddy sat reading, apparently oblivious of background
music. He had fair, curly hair, a pale face—everyone in
Millways had that, anyhow—and bright blue eyes. He was
beginning to irritate Benson a little, because he didn't talk
much either and even in these circumstances could become absorbed in a book. Benson wasn't one for much
reading, and there were no old newspapers in the house.
Freddy had never smoked, but Benson had an unbearable
craving for a cigarette. To make it worse, Benson could
have had tobacco, but had forgotten to bring any away
with him. There were two pounds of it in his cell! The
ruddy screws would get it now, and they'd swear they
didn't know he had it. They might not even tell the
Governor, might just pass it on to one of the trusties and
get a cut in the proceeds.

Freddy flipped over a page.

"Freddy," Benson said, "we've got to eat."

Freddy glanced up. "S'right," he said.

"It's nearly dark outside. Must be."

"Got to wait until it's pitch." Freddy was obviously
impatient to get back to his book. "Got to find some food
that won't be missed. That shop at the corner'll be okay,
but it won't close until six. Got to wait until half past six,
anyway."

He was right, of course; there was nothing of the fool about him. He was good, and he had a strong nerve. He would go out and break into the shop, and Benson knew he could trust him. But Benson didn't like his cocksure manner.

Freddy turned back to his book. Now and again he grinned, now and again he read so fast that his eyes seemed to swivel to and fro in his head. All that Benson knew was that the book was a Western—and that Freddy might soon begin to get on his nerves.

He got up and went out of the room, going from room to room everywhere in the house. It was still daylight outside, and the sky was gray, but it wasn't snowing. Snow had been swept from the middle of the road and packed into great banks on either side. Lights were on at several houses. Children were snowballing, some with furious enjoyment. In sight of the front-room window, which Benson approached cautiously from one side, there were three snowmen, each in a tiny front garden. Everywhere it was gently quiet, and even the children's voices did not sound through the closed and latched windows.

Benson went downstairs again and sat for a while until, without looking up, Freddy stretched out a hand and pressed a different button on the radio. The music stopped; instead, a man was talking about the weather. Benson opened his mouth to ask: "What's that for?" and then realized why Freddy had changed the station. The news would be on the Home Service in a minute or two, and they would be "news" with a vengeance. He forgot his momentary annoyance because Freddy was so self-sufficient.

The weather report ended, and the Greenwich time signal came: Peeep, peeep, peeep, peeep, peeep, peeep. At last Freddy put down his book. Both men leaned nearer to the radio, which was tuned very low, so that the voice was only a whisper. Foreign news, Parliamentary news, a Royal visit, all of these came in headlines. And finally:

"Three of the nine convicts who escaped fromMillways Prison early this morning have been recaptured, two of them within half a mile of the prison walls, the third as he attempted to obtain clothes from a secondhand shop on the outskirts of Manchester."

Benson and Freddy looked at each other, now equally tense. Details would be given later, they would have to listen to all the other news before learning which of the three had been caught. Benson's nerves were at screaming point, but at least Freddy Tisdale didn't go back to his book. Once the news was over, it would be dark enough to go and get some food.

As he waited, Benson knew how sick hunger could make a man feel.

5 . The Primrose Girl

Gideon hadn't been able to go straight to H5 Division and see young Rose. Two things had come in, while he had been talking to Mary: a smash-and-grab job in Soho, and a panic about a Foreign Office man who was missing from his home and his office. The F.O. job was rightly the Special Branch's; but everyone was sensitive to the antics of diplomats, and Gideon had hurried along to a hastily summoned conference with the A.C., the Special Branch Chief, and a Foreign Office representative for whom Gideon had little time. He had hardly got back to his office when his telephone bell rang, and he lifted the receiver as he reached his desk.

"Gideon."

"Excuse me, sir," a man said, "this is Detective-Sergeant Cummings. I'm with the gentleman from the Public Prosecutor's office, and there are a few matters I'd be grateful for your advice on."

"Hmm," grunted Gideon.

"If we could come along for five minutes, sir."

"All right, I'll be here," said Gideon. He put the receiver down, scowled, and told Lemaitre what it was. For once he didn't find himself smiling when his C.I. said:

"These new P.P. barristers get on my wick, twice as much trouble as they're worth. Should have thought Cummings could have handled this chap, though."

Gideon said, "They can't all have your brilliance, can they? Did you fix everything for Benson's wife, and all the rest?"

"All done. Sent Old Percy and a youngster to Mrs. B's—Abbott. You remember, he jumped on a car and nearly won himself an early coffin."

"Divisions take it seriously?"

"Everyone takes Benson seriously," Lemaitre said. "Mind if I give you a word of advice, George?"

Lemaitre grinned as he said that. His lean face, with its

rather leathery, hungry look, had a drollness which couldn't be missed; and when he grinned it was with one side of his mouth and with one eye screwed up a little—this because he so often had a cigarette dangling from the corner of his lips. He hadn't now, but the mannerism remained. He had sleek, almost jet-black hair, which was brushed back from his forehead without a parting; and although he was as old as Gideon, there was hardly a gray strand except at the temples and the back of his neck. His eyes were brown, restless, and very bright, and he was always on the move. Take his one big drawback away, and he might become brilliant. There wasn't a better man at the Yard on routine, and whatever the situation, there wasn't a man who knew how to get things moving more quickly than Lemaitre, or who could move faster. He was the ideal second-in-command.

Gideon kept a straight face.

"I'm always ready to take advice from my betters," he said.

"And learning, too," marveled Lemaitre. "I know, I know, you'll tell me to keep my big mouth shut, but here it comes. Don't waste your time on the Primrose Girl job, you're going to have plenty to do over this Millways job. Give you three to one that before the afternoon's out we'll have a conference with the Home Office; you know what they're like on a case like this. And if you're not sitting at the end of a telephone, you'll rile everyone except the A.C., and perhaps even him if the Commissioner gets narky."

"Lem, you couldn't be more right," said Gideon.

Before they could say any more, Cummings and a bright-eyed, fresh-faced young man from the Public Prosecutor's office came in. If anything was certain, it was that the P.P.'s man was not being officious. He looked competent, intelligent and amiable, and there was no long-suffering air about Cummings, either. This was a genuine problem about the case against Edmundsun. Within two minutes, Gideon had shaken hands with the barrister, whose name was Harrison, and had put everything out of his mind except the embezzlement case. The prosecution's main hopes lay in one police witness; the great weakness, that the witness might be shaken by the defense. Young Harrison said that he'd read all the statements and studied the witness's statements, and was sure that the defense couldn't shake the witness, who was vulnerable on two points. How could they block the defense?

The session, interrupted by four telephone calls, lasted for over an hour. Cummings, a youngish man who ran to fat, and whose face and forehead were shiny all the time, had a complete grasp of the intricate case; Harrison seemed to have it all under his hat, too. Gideon knew that he had seen the man before, but couldn't say where; probably in court, when the police had been there in strength.

They all stood up, at a little before one o'clock.

"Better have a day to think this over," Harrison said, "we don't want to put Edmundsun in court and see him wriggle out."

"Give me a ring, and we'll have another look at it tomorrow," Gideon offered.

"Thanks," said Harrison, and then gave a boyish grin. He was public school, probably Oxford; he dressed immaculately and expensively, and he got on as well with ex-elementary schoolboy Cummings as he would with the Home Secretary in person. "Mind if I say it's been nice meeting you? The only time we've met before, you made mincemeat out of me."

"I did?" Gideon couldn't recall any encounter with him. "Where?"

"Number One Court at the Old Bailey," Harrison said. "I was junior counsel for the defense of Sydney Benson, and my leader had been called out. I opened my mouth, and you put your foot in it! Never felt smaller in my life—and never been so wrong," Harrison went on, earnestly. "I hear that Benson's one of the crowd to escape from Millways. That ought to make everyone happy—except perhaps his wife."

This man was no fool; in a few years he would probably be a big name; and he could be human enough to think anxiously about Benson's wife.

He went on very slowly: "I was very green in those days, almost believed that Benson was innocent and the police were perjuring themselves, until I saw the way he looked at his wife when she gave evidence. Remember the way he spoke to her, just before she stood down?" Harrison hesitated, then tightened his lips and spoke so that they hardly moved: a good imitation of Benson's way of speaking. " 'Okay, Ruby, I'll pay you for this.' If he'd threatened to slit her throat he couldn't have sounded worse."

Gideon said, "So that's where I've seen you. Well, don't worry about Ruby Benson, we're looking after her."

"I didn't need to ask!"

Gideon grinned. "Think we can't take a hint? How about coming down to the canteen for a meal?" he added. "Or we could go across to the pub."

"Wish I could, but I've got to get back," Harrison said. "Seen anything of Ruby Benson since the trial? I used to wonder if she let Benson down because there was a boy friend waiting until he went inside."

"It's a funny thing," Gideon told him, "but I heard something about her only a few weeks ago. She's been working so as to keep the two kids going; made out all right, too. Assistant in a gown shop. Recently she found a boy friend, and you know what suspicious minds we coppers have. The G5 Divisional chaps made sure that she'd never met the man before. He took over management of the shop where she works, only a few months ago."

"What a future," mused Harrison, slowly. "Husband in jail, and when he comes out he's likely to kill you. Work to keep your children decent, have a boy friend who hasn't a chance of marrying you for twelve years or more, and probably not then. Why can't it work out as badly as that for Benson?" That seemed no more than a casual remark, and Harrison went toward the door, adding, "Know any of the other men who escaped?"

"Only one," said Gideon. "Jingo Smith. The others got into jail without any help from me."

He shook hands, nodded to Cummings, who looked pleased with himself, then went back into the office. Lemaitre, who hadn't shown any outward interest in what had gone on, but who had undoubtedly heard everything, glanced up to speak. Before he could, one of three telephones on his desk rang; he plucked it up as the ringing reached full blast.

"Lemaitre . . . Okay, that's fine, ta." He rang off, almost in the same motion with which he had lifted the instrument, and said quite casually, "They've picked up the chap for that hit-and-run job in Battersea; commercial traveler who lives at Brixton. Blood on the mudguard and tires. Better just leave it to the Division, hadn't I?"

"Yes," said Gideon. "You hungry?"

Lemaitre looked suspicious. "What's this?"

"We could send for a couple of sandwiches," said Gideon.

"When it's your public school pals, you take 'em to the pub and stand 'em a meal," Lemaitre jeered, "but your real friends . . ."

Gideon's telephone rang.

Gideon moved toward it, while Lemaitre was still speaking.

"I suppose you want to get all the desk work done so that you can go and see H5 this afternoon. Fat lot of use giving you advice! But you'll regret it, George; I can smell a busy day, and—oh, hell. But what did I tell you?"

One of his telephones was ringing.

"Lemaitre," he barked.

Gideon picked up his own receiver. He did that as he did nearly everything: with an outward appearance of slowness, as if he were giving himself plenty of time to think. It was simply that he had learned not to rush at anything, except in dire emergency, and even then it often did more harm than good. He put the receiver to his ear, and looked thoughtfully across at Lemaitre, who was snapping briskly.

"Gideon," said Gideon.

"Your wife's on the line, Mr. Gideon," a girl operator said; "I told her I thought you were in."

Gideon didn't answer at once; he really needed a moment to get used to the idea that Kate had telephoned him. It was utterly unexpected. He couldn't recall her doing so for years, except in real emergency. That was the result of the early, bitter estrangement between them, and it had grown into habit. Would Kate ring now unless something was the matter?

With Pru, Priscilla, Penny, one of the boys?

"Put her through."

"Yes, sir."

Gideon was kept waiting only a few seconds, but his heart was beating faster than it should. Lemaitre was now barking into his telephone, but Gideon made no attempt to follow what he was saying, just tried to reassure himself about this call. Then Kate came on the line. He couldn't tell from her voice whether she was really worried or not; she was a remarkable woman for controlling her emotions.

"Hallo, George, I'm glad I've caught you," she said; "I promised Pru that I'd have a word with you. This isn't a bad time, is it?"

"Promised Pru—" began Gideon, and then relaxed and grinned broadly. "You tell that daughter of mine that when she wants to plead for a young man accused of murder, she'd better come and see me herself, not work through her mother."

Kate said, as if astounded, "How on *earth* did you know?" Then she gave a little laugh, almost one of confusion. "I always understood you were good at your job, but not . . ."

"Tell you about it when I get home," said Gideon. "But you can tell Pru that I shall be seeing young Rose this afternoon, or early this evening, and you can also remind her that we still prefer to let the innocent ones go."

He didn't attempt to keep the chuckle out of his voice. Nor did Kate.

"That'll cheer her up no end," she said. "She read about it in a midday paper; apparently the boy's sister used to be at the school with her."

"That boy's sister is worth cultivating," said Gideon. "She bearded this lion in his den. Kate, I'm sorry but I ought to get off the line, it's building up to quite a day. I'll get home as early as I can."

"I can guess how early," Kate said dryly. "Good-by, dear." And then, in the same breath, "Have you caught Benson yet?"

"No, but we will," said Gideon, quietly. "By."

He rang off.

Lemaitre was still on the telephone, but scribbling notes; he could write at furious speed and still be neat. The office was now pleasantly warm, and the sun had broken through; spring was here with a vengeance. Vengeance. Spring, and Sydney Benson out of jail, his wife aware of it by now, other desperate men at liberty, and—frightened people. Mary Rose, her brother, her mother, even Pru. Ruby Benson, and perhaps this new boy friend of hers. And who else?

"We will," he'd told Kate, meaning that they would soon catch Benson and all the others, but—would they? It couldn't be much more important.

Lemaitre snapped into the telephone, "Okay, do that." He put down the telephone, and looked across at Gideon; and for a moment Gideon had a feeling that he was also touched with fear.

"Still caught only three," Lemaitre said; "we'd better soon have the rest, or we'll really go to town. Man saw two of them in a railway shed up in Lancaster. He went after them on his own, and they bashed him with lumps of coal. On the danger list. They're checking the coal for prints, don't know which of the six it was, yet, but that's the kind of thing Benson would do, and if they're going to try to stay clear at all costs—well, I can't say I like it."

Gideon said, "I'm holding my sides. Who'd they catch for Number 3? I only knew it wasn't Benson."

"Nicky Bown."

"Did he say anything?"

"Not much, but he did say that the others are in pairs: Jingo Smith with Matt Owens, Wally Alderman with Hooky, and Benson with a youngster named Tisdale, double-jointed customer who helped to beat up a night watchman. Nice setup. One really tough guy in each pair, and you can be pretty sure they've all gone in different directions. Anything more we can do, do you think?"

"Every man we've got is alerted," said Gideon. "So, there isn't, yet. I . . ."

The telephone behind him rang.

It was too often like this: no pause between one thing and another, no time to get his mind fixed on a problem before he had to switch to the next. Today was worse than usual, or else he was noticing it more. The intrusion of Mary Rose, Pru and Kate were factors he wouldn't normally have to deal with, and he was more worried than he showed about Benson's escape. The man who didn't respect Benson's ability was a fool.

He picked up the receiver.

"Gideon."

"George," said a superintendent named Wrexall, "I've got Ruby Benson on the line, but she'd like a word with you. Can do?"

In the past half hour, several things had happened in London that Gideon didn't know about:

In New Bond Street, only a stone's throw from the police station at Savile Row, a small sports car drew up outside a jeweler's shop, a young man got out and calmly smashed a plate-glass window with a big hammer. The noise was so loud that it sounded like a car crash. As the window fell outward, two other men ran toward it, each carrying a sack with a wide, hooped opening. They grabbed silver, gold, jewels, everything in sight; and, as they did so, the man who had smashed the window tossed smoke bombs among the crowd. In ninety seconds, it was all over. The men ran back to the sports car, which roared along the road, the driver ignoring a point duty policeman, who leaped for his life.

As the car swung round the corner, another policeman leaped at it and tried to get at the steering wheel. One thief smashed at his head, another at his hands, but he didn't let go. The car swerved, mounted the pavement, and crashed.

The policeman wasn't seriously injured.

A few miles away, a young constable, hearing cries for help, peered over Putney Bridge and saw a woman and a child struggling in the river. He spoke calmly to two passersby as he stripped off his tunic, put his helmet on the parapet, and dived into the water. He saved both woman and child.

The third thing was not so spectacular. A constable, doing his usual rounds, noticed a familiar face coming out of a big building in Norton Square, W.1. The face was of one of London's most notorious safebreakers, not long out of jail. This man, Lefty Bligh, was known to spy out the lay of the land thoroughly before he did a job.

The constable made his report about this by telephone to his sergeant, who was soon talking to the Yard.

6 . Benson's Wife

Whenever he had a mental picture of Syd Benson's wife, Gideon saw a woman in her early thirties, with a figure that a girl of twenty might have envied, and the face of a woman of middle age. It was a sad face, much more sad than anything else, as of one who had given up expecting anything at all from life. During the time of Benson's remand before his trial, Gideon had often talked to her. Every now and again something had animated her, and she'd shown a glimpse of the beauty she was known to have been; but it was faded, as a dying flower. Even at thirty-three, her hair had been liberally streaked with gray.

As Gideon waited for her to come through, that was the picture he had of her.

Then: "You're through," said the operator.

"Hallo, Mrs. Benson," Gideon said quietly.

"Is that"—a pause—"is that Superintendent Gideon?"

"Superintendent" would do, that was how she had known him.

"Yes, speaking. If you're worried about the two men I've stationed—"

"No, it's not about them," interrupted Ruby Benson, in a voice which suggested that she was more agitated than she wanted him to know. "I was told about Syd early this morning, and I expected you to send someone. But I'm not worried about myself, Mr. Gideon."

Boy friend?

"Who are you worried about?"

"The children," she said flatly, "and I really mean that, Mr. Gideon." He could believe her; and he forgot that he had even thought "boy friend." "You're the one man I needn't be afraid to talk to," she went on; "you know Syd, and you know what he can do. I've been thinking it out, Mr. Gideon: I've often wondered what he'd do if he did get a chance, and I don't believe he'd go for me. I think he'd get at me through the children. Until he's caught, I don't want them living at home with me, I wouldn't feel safe."

Gideon said, "Listen, Mrs. Benson, you've nothing at all to worry about today. Syd can't get to London in weather like they've got up north—there's little traffic about on the roads, watching is easy as kiss your hand. So there's no immediate worry. You going to be in this aftenoon and this evening?"

"Well, yes," she said.

"I'll come and have a word with you, but I can't promise when," said Gideon. "Not before half past four, anyhow. And if you're worried about the children today, in spite of what I've told you, I'll arrange for a man to go to their school and—"

"No, it's all right today," Ruby Benson said quickly, and her relief sent her voice two octaves higher. "Thanks ever so much, Mr. Gideon. I'll wait in."

She rang off.

She had never had very much to say, and Gideon had often wondered what she really felt and thought. At one time it had seemed as if the years with Benson had cowed her, but she had shown great courage when she had turned on him. Just now, the sudden relief and the vitality in her voice had surprised him.

He pushed his chair back.

"Sandwiches coming up," Lemaitre said. "Going lady-killing today, eh?"

"That's it."

"Well, don't say I didn't warn you," Lemaitre said. "You heard about that chap who stopped the smash-and-grab job?"

"No. Hurt?"

"They didn't detain him in hospital, he's being taken home. Ought to get a medal, he jumped a car while it was doing fifty."

"Then he'll probably get his medal."

"Good day for heroes," Lemaitre said, with a grimace. "Chap out at Putney dived into the Thames and saved a woman who'd jumped in after her kid—kid had fallen in from the towpath."

Gideon felt a warming glow.

"Get me his name and number, will you?"

"It's on the way. There's another thing we ought to do something about," Lemaitre went on with a sniff. "Lefty Bligh's around again, seen coming out of the Carfax Building in Merton Square. What do you make of that?"

Gideon said quietly, "Find out just where he was, Lem. Send someone who knows his habits. Find out if there's anything worth pinching kept in the place, and lay on everything that's needed."

Lemaitre nodded.

It was nearly four o'clock before Gideon left the Yard. He went alone, driving the black Wolseley, and the bright afternoon sunshine showed up the little scratches, the dust and the smears on the glass and the bodywork. He didn't drive fast. He let his thoughts roam over every inquiry that was going through the Yard, and hoped that nothing big would break for a day or two, but he wasn't too sanguine; big things were always liable to break, and they had a trick of coming two or three at a time. Strictly speaking, catching Benson wasn't a Yard job and wouldn't be until there was proof that the man was in the London Metropolitan area, but Benson was Case Number 1.

Case Number 2 was the Primrose Girl.

Gideon had looked through the afternoon newspapers before leaving the office. The mass escape from Millways had driven the Primrose Girl off the main headlines, but there was the story of the arrest of William Rose and a picture of the boy. The telling of the story was typical of Fleet Street: no direct statement that Rose was guilty, nothing that might at any time be construed as contempt of court, but the facts were stated in such a way that nine readers out of ten would feel sure that William Rose was the murderer. The Divisional police had told the Press plenty, including the bit about the boy's penknife; they'd said more than Gideon would have done, so early as this. H5 Division was worrying him, and would soon become an anxiety.

The world would soon think the boy guilty.

And Mary Rose either knew that he was innocent, or was prepared to lie desperately to save him.

To reach H5 he had to cross the river; it was Lambeth way. He drove faster as he got out of the thick London traffic, and it was half past four when he reached the sprawling building which housed the H5 Divisional Headquarters. The district was drab, most of the houses near it were small, and many wanted painting; taken by and large, it was a depressing area. Gideon knew that the Roses lived some distance from here, in a new—well, newish—estate.

He hadn't told H5 that he was going; only Lemaitre knew. That was because he didn't want everything brushed up and made shiny for him. Within two minutes of stepping into the low-ceilinged hall, however, he wondered if he'd made a mistake. The desk sergeant, recognizing him at the first glance and coming almost to attention, told him that the Superintendent had gone home early.

"Got a shocking cold he had, sir."

"Oh. Lot of them about," said Gideon. "Who's in charge?"

"Chief Inspector Smedd, sir."

"Tell him I'm on my way, will you?"

"Yes, sir," said the sergeant. "Right away."

Gideon didn't hurry. The old building had a lot of steep stone steps, and he knew from experience that if he didn't take it carefully he would be breathless when he reached the second floor; and it wasn't good policy to be puffing and blowing in front of the men up there. He now knew that Smedd was the officer who had arrested young Rose, and he knew Smedd well enough to realize that he was quite capable of brushing Mary Rose off. He was a go-getter, and he was a damned good detective and almost as good a policeman; they didn't always mean the same thing. He wasn't a man whom Gideon liked, but they had never clashed. Taken by and large, if Smedd said that a thing was true, it was.

Smedd was at the open door of the Superintendent's room, which he shared with the Superintendent; and Gideon wondered how often the senior man went home early.

"Hallo, Commander—unexpected honor," said Smedd, and gave a fierce smile and offered a vigorous handshake. He was on the small side for a C.I.D. man and, in his early days, must have scraped in by the better part of a hair's breadth, although the five feet ten rule had been relaxed for a long time now. He was dressed in brown, the color just a trifle on the bright side; his tie was colorful; his crisp, almost ginger hair was very oily. He had a raw look: a scrubbed look, rather. His skin was very fresh, and, especially at his nose and eyes, was a mass of freckles. "Come in—sorry the Superintendent's not here, he packed up early. Sneezing all over the place. You kept clear of colds this winter?"

"Pretty clear, thanks."

"Good. Sit down. How about a cuppa? Had one myself, but never say no, you know."

"I won't, thanks," said Gideon. "Lemaitre poured a cup into me before I left." He sat down and looked about him, and knew, even then, that the Superintendent might spend a lot of time at the station, but he had really given way to Smedd; for this place was spick-and-span, everything was in its proper place. Even the Superintendent's roll-top desk, usually a litter of papers, was as neat as the rest of it. Since Gideon had last been here, there had been a new, bigger, flat-topped desk brought in, too. Smedd's?

Smedd went and sat behind it.

"Come about the Primrose Girl job, I suppose. Glad we didn't take long to get the young swine. Kind I'd hang if I had my way.

"Hmm," said Gideon. "Nasty job. Sure he did it, I suppose?" He didn't smile. "Had a morning session with a man from the P.P.'s office, and the chief moan was that I'd put up a case which might not stand up in court, so I'm sensitive."

"Oh, we'll get Rose," Smedd said.

Gideon didn't comment.

Smedd frowned. A quick-tempered man at best, he wouldn't give way to his temper with Gideon, but neither would he be able to hide the fact that he felt annoyed, or at least impatient.

"I'd take the case to court tomorrow. Asking for a week, of course, if that's okay with you; we might as well get it all sewn up before we commit him for trial, but there isn't a shred of doubt. Talking off the cuff, of course, wouldn't say this to the P.P.'s office yet, but—haven't you studied the report I sent in?"

Reproof.

Gideon said, "Yes, but let me have the main points again, will you?"

Smedd's look said, jeeringly, "I'll bet you've read it—I don't think!" He didn't speak at once, but opened a drawer and took out a foolscap-sized manila folder, opened this, and showed a sheaf of papers clipped together; perhaps twenty sheets of paper, some large, some small, some handwritten, some typewritten. He began to read from a typewritten sheet on the top, without looking at Gideon, but giving the impression that he preferred facts to speak for themselves.

"Rose and Winifred Norton had been keeping company for six months. She was always at his house, or he was always at hers. The only quarrels we can find were because he was jealous—he hated her to be seen with other men." Smedd sneered the "men." "Recently, she'd been more interested in other men than in Rose. They had a violent quarrel a few hours before she was found murdered. She went to gather primroses, after the quarrel, and—"

"By herself?" interposed Gideon.

"Yes. She told a girl friend where she was going, and said it was to get away from Rose; she was nervous of him. That's the last time she was seen alive. The body was found the following morning, some primroses clutched in her left hand, eleven stab wounds, mostly in the breast. If you ask me, the boy's a monster." Whatever else, Smedd was convinced of that; the words spat out from his lips. "Those are the facts about her. After the quarrel, Rose wandered about on his own. He didn't go home. He didn't go to her home. He says he went to the pictures, but his footprints were found near the body, his knife was found among the primroses, with some of his prints on it, the blade was smeared with blood. She was stabbed through her clothes, so no blood splashed or spurted, and there was none on his clothes or hands," Smedd went on very quickly, "but we don't need that for evidence. Take it from me, we've got that young swine where we want him."

Smedd broke off, as if challenging Gideon to deny it.

"How does Rose explain his knife?"

"Usual story: he lost it, a day or two ago."

"His footprints?"

"Oh, he admits he saw the girl there, but says he left her. And so he did—dead," Smedd added, and the challenge in his manner became even more aggressive.

7 . Ruby Benson

Gideon had known from the beginning that it would be as difficult to shift Smedd from an opinion as it would to shift Lemaitre. He knew more: Smedd had done a great number of things he hadn't mentioned. He might have overlooked something, but for the most part he would have done a thorough job. And if he, Gideon, started to check, he would only be putting Smedd's back further up, which would help no one. So Gideon did what he would have done with a man whom he knew better and whom he liked. He nodded, in that almost ponderous way of his, and took out his big-bowled pipe. He found himself smoking less and less these days, and then mostly in the evenings. Now, he began to fill the big bowl; and he gave a slow, rueful smile, which obviously puzzled Smedd.

"Well, you've got it all sewn up," Gideon said. "I didn't have much doubt that you would. Pity."

Smedd's green-brown eyes could not have been brighter.

"Pity?" he ejaculated. "Goddamnit, what else do you want?" So he could unbend enough under pressure. "The swine has a row with his girl friend, nice, clean-living girl, only just beginning to spread her wings. Virgin, too—at least he didn't try to interfere with her. She tells him it's the end, so what does he do? Follows her into the woods and then kills her with his knife, stabbing her nearly a dozen times. He must have lost his temper until he was almost mad, and that's what the defense will try of course —insanity plea. But he's no more mad than I am. He's just like a lot of the young swine these days. All right while he gets what he wants, but as soon as something gets in his way he loses his head. And you say it's a pity!"

Smedd paused.

Gideon was still smiling, ruefully, almost apologetically; and now he had finished filling his pipe. There were a few tricks Smedd didn't know yet, and one of them was that Gideon liked the other man to do most of the talking, especially at times like this. Smedd might keep quiet long enough to force him to comment, or he might not have the patience.

Smedd put both hands together, clenching them tightly.

"Don't tell me that you're starting to sympathize with a young brute like this just because you've got kids of your own. I've got three, remember."

Gideon spoke at last. "No, it's not that, although that comes into it in a way. Funny thing, but young Rose's sister, the one named Mary, knows my daughter Pru. Studied music together, or something. So I promised I'd see if there was a weak spot anywhere. I had a sneaking hope you might not be quite certain that it was this Rose boy. Still, nothing to be done, obviously." He paused. "Mind if I have a word with Rose?"

"Sure, have a word when you like," Smedd said. "He won't fool you any more than he did me. See his sister?"

"She stormed the Yard!"

"She tried to storm in here," Smedd told him, thinly, "but I don't stand any nonsense from the kids who think they know everything. And I don't intend to let anyone call me a liar, even if she is a girl who's a bit worked up."

Gideon made a whistling sound.

"She do that?"

"Oh, and a lot more hysterical nonsense," Smedd said tartly. "Either hysteria, or she was trying it on. Anyhow, what we have to work on are the *facts*." He patted the file of papers. "And in that file there are enough facts to convict him twice over. Only worry I've got is this insanity plea. Every time a kid gets off on that, I think that two others will probably kill in the same way, believing they might get away with it. Funny thing, the human mind. Subconscious has a hell of a lot to answer for."

"I'll say it does," said Gideon. "No weak spots, apart from that?"

"No." Smedd gripped his hands again tightly. "I've seen every member of the staff who works at the cinema where Rose's sister says they went, and had them look at

Rose's photograph. None of them recognized him. Don't get me wrong," Smedd went on. "I don't believe the sister, but her story had to be checked, even if it was wasting the time of men who were needed on a more useful job. If she sticks to her story, the defense will try to prove that they did go to that cinema, but I've made sure before they start snooping."

"Couldn't be tighter," said Gideon.

"No, it couldn't be."

"Hardly worth my talking to him," said Gideon; "but you know what it's like with these youngsters, I won't get any peace at home until I've been able to say that I've talked to Rose myself."

"Let's go and see him," said Smedd. "I had a word with the A.C. about the advisability of a special court this afternoon, but he agreed that we could wait until the morning. Gave me time to check everything while making sure that the young brute didn't start running, or do any more damage."

"Hmm," said Gideon.

They went downstairs. The cells at the H5 station were in a semi-basement with frosted glass windows and bars; a gloomy, dingy place, quite enough to work on the fears of an innocent man. A sergeant was on duty at a desk. He straightened up when Smedd appeared, then recognized Gideon.

"We're going to see Rose," Smedd said.

"Yes, sir."

Gideon, effacing himself in a way which was remarkable for so large a man, followed the other two along a narrow corridor toward the cells. He wasn't really affected by Mary Rose's plea, but he found himself thinking about young Rose in a way that Smedd certainly wouldn't approve. Here was a boy, aged twenty, with all life before him; and upstairs, in between two thin covers, were twenty or more years in prison. But supposing he was innocent? What was going on in his mind, his sister's, his mother's?

William Rose heard them coming, and stood up as they reached the cell. He was smaller than Gideon had expected, slender and pale. If Gideon had been told that he was sixteen, he wouldn't have been surprised. He was remarkably like his sister, but his coloring was different; he was fair when she was dark, and his eyes were sky blue, a color picked out by the strip lighting. He wore a gray suit, his hair was neatly done, his shoes were polished; a young man who took care of himself.

Smedd barked, "This is Commander Gideon, of New Scotland Yard."

William Rose said quietly, "How're you, sir."

There was a hopeless look about him, which was apparent at once. Gideon had seen it often before, and it was no indication of guilt or innocence. Everything now happening was so utterly different from his normal life, and he felt lost.

Gideon said, "Evening, Rose. Sorry to find you in this predicament." That was the last approach that the boy expected—or Smedd, for that matter. "I don't know how much Chief Inspector Smedd has told you, but you know that in English law you've got a right to a defense, and the right to be regarded as innocent unless you're proved guilty."

The boy said, "That's all very well in theory, sir."

So he wasn't cowed, yet.

"What do you mean, exactly?" asked Gideon, in his slow, quiet way, and his placid expression could have done nothing to make the boy feel worse.

"There isn't a man here who treats me as if I was innocent; they've all jumped to the conclusion that I'm guilty." As he spoke, Rose looked at Smedd; not bitterly, but doggedly.

"Well, aren't you?" Gideon asked, still in that deceptively mild voice.

William Rose said, "I did not kill Winifred, sir, and I know nothing about it. I lost my knife several days ago, and the killer must have found it. I went to the pictures with my sister Mary, after Winifred and I had quarreled. That's the truth, sir."

Gideon was watching steadily. He said, "Know where you lost the knife?"

"No, sir."

"Told anyone else you'd lost it?"

The boy colored.

"No, sir, I didn't. It was a birthday present from my sister Mary, and I hoped I wouldn't have to tell her—or the family."

"Hm. All right, Rose, if you've told the truth, we'll prove it. Won't we, Chief Inspector?"

"We'll certainly establish the truth," Smedd said flatly.

"And that's all anyone wants," Gideon said. "Chief Inspector, I wonder if you could send a shorthand writer here, and let me ask Rose a few questions. Mind?"

Smedd couldn't very well refuse.

Gideon put the questions, mildly, in a manner much more friendly than hostile. The answers came out sharply at first, as if the boy was aware that he was fighting a losing battle. Gradually his tension eased, and he spoke more naturally; by the time the questions were over, he was speaking eagerly and with color in his cheeks.

His statement to Gideon coincided in every detail with two statements he had made earlier. If he was lying, nothing revealed itself by discrepancies in what he said.

"Thanks very much, Smedd," Gideon said, at the door of the police station, as they shook hands. "Sorry to poke my nose in, but you know how these things are. And with youngsters these days, people are so touchy—want to wrap them up in cotton wool. I daren't take a chance that something might have slipped up here; if it had, we'd be in for real trouble. And just between you and me . . ."

He stopped.

He knew exactly what he was saying and what he was doing, but Smedd didn't realize that. Smedd was agog for a confidence. It didn't come for a long time, and when it did it seemed to be almost with embarrassment.

"Keep this to yourself, won't you, Smedd, but there's a rumor that the A.C. might resign at the end of the year. Come into some private money, I hear. And you can't blame me for keeping an eye on the main chance, can you? Surprising how a 'not guilty' verdict rankles in the Home Office mind. One or two would be quite enough for them to pass me over. What with that and my daughter's personal interest—but I've got to be off!"

Smedd watched him go.

Smedd, who knew that Gideon's recommendation was the only thing he needed to be next in line for the superintendency at H5, was almost certainly checking over every detail in his mind, more determined than ever not to slip up. He would test the weakness in his case as thoroughly as any defending lawyer; there was no more risk that he would steam-roller over young William Rose.

Nice boy.

Nice boys sometimes had uncontrollable tempers, and

Rose had owned the knife which had killed the Primrose Girl.

It was a quarter to six when Gideon's car turned into narrow, drab Muskett Street, where Mrs. Benson lived. At a corner of the street leading to it, he had seen Old Percy, one of the senior detective sergeants at the Yard—a sergeant because of seniority only; he was utterly lacking in ambition. Percy was a biggish man, with a big stomach; he had won the Metropolitan Police boxing championship for six years in a row, and still had the strength of an ox. One of the soundest men the Yard was ever likely to have, he recognized Gideon but didn't bat an eye.

He was watching the back of the house.

Young Abbott was at the front.

The detective officer was walking toward the car, and was almost level with Number 52, where Ruby Benson lived. He walked with long, deliberate strides, and looked as if he might have given Old Percy a run for his money had they been of an age in Percy's boxing days. Abbott walked more like a policeman on beat duty than a plain-clothes man watching a house—and it would be a long time before he got rid of that walk. Gideon had no particular objection to it; there were times when it was an advantage for a C.I.D. man to look like a policeman. He'd grow out of it, anyway.

Gideon drew up.

Abbott peered at him, saw who it was, and jumped forward to open the door.

"Afternoon, sir!"

"Hallo," said Gideon, as if surprised. "You on this job?"

"I'm being relieved at eight o'clock, sir. Sergeant Lawson—"

"I've seen him," said Gideon. "Anything happened to worry either of you?"

"Nothing at all's worried me, sir." Abbott reported the comings and goings of the Benson children and of two people who lived upstairs in this small house; and gave the description of two callers, one man and one woman, neither of whom had gone inside. Uneventful was the word. Gideon turned toward the house and saw a curtain move; either Ruby Benson or the children were peeping at him. As he reached the front door, he noticed the children inside the little front room: a boy of twelve and a girl of ten. He knocked. The children shouted something, their mother called to them sharply, and there was a scuffle of footsteps. Then Ruby Benson opened the door.

Gideon had a shock.

This was Ruby Benson all right, but she looked unbelievably younger. Changes in people so often had the opposite effect that this was astonishing. It was like looking at her younger sister. Of course she had her hair touched up, and it was no longer gray at the sides; the gray streak in the front was gone, too; but her youthfulness wasn't just due to her hair. Her skin looked clearer, her eyes had lost the long-suffering look he had known before. He could swear that she had fewer wrinkles, too. She was neatly made up, and her eyes were very bright. She wore a white blouse and a dark-gray skirt, and her figure was still the figure of a girl in her early twenties.

Gideon put out his hand.

"Well, well," he said, "you must tell me how you do it. I wouldn't mind knocking ten years off my age, too."

It pleased her, and she smiled. Her teeth were very even, so even that they were probably false, but that didn't matter. She shook hands hesitantly, then stood aside to let him in.

"I don't have the worry that I used to have—well, I didn't until today," she said. "The front room." Gideon knew the front room, turned into it, and had his second surprise. It had been redecorated throughout, it looked larger, and the freshness was in sharp contrast to the district. "Bit different since you were here last, isn't it?" she asked, and followed him in and closed the door. "It—it's ever so good of you to come. They haven't got him yet, have they?" That came quickly, revealing the anxiety so close to the surface.

"Not yet," Gideon had to agree.

"I've got a funny feeling," Benson's wife said abruptly. "I've got a feeling that he'll get down here, Mr. Gideon, and that he'll have a go at the kids. Like I told you. He knows they mean more to me than anything else, and it would just about suit him, that would—knowing I was alive and the kids were dead or—well, crippled or something. There's something I didn't ever tell you," she went on, speaking much too quickly, as she had done over the telephone. "His mother went to see him in Millways, did you know that?"

"No."

"Well, she did. And when she came back, she told me

what he'd said to her. He gave her a message, actually, and she didn't understand it. But I did. I didn't tell her, and I didn't tell anyone; but—well, when I heard about Syd escaping, it came over me, Mr. Gideon. I could hardly think because I was so scared."

He could believe her.

"What was it?" he asked.

She said: "He told me to remember what had happened to the Micklewright family. Just that. You wouldn't know them, I shouldn't think. They were pals of Syd's, years ago, and Micklewright used to do jobs for him. He thought Syd pulled a fast one over him. I didn't know for sure but I was always afraid that Syd had done it. Now I know."

Gideon didn't tell her that she was almost incoherent. He could see how she had been bottling this up inside her; and now it was bursting out, and when it was all over she would feel better. He could see the outline of the picture that she was drawing, too.

She went on:

"The Micklewrights had two kids, see, and they were hit by a car, hit-and-run it was. They were with Micklewright, with their dad. He was killed, and so was one of the kids, and the other's been a cripple ever since. I couldn't ever be sure that Syd had done that; all I knew was that Micklewright died, and—and what had happened to the kids. Then when Syd's mother gave me the message, well—what could I think except what I did?"

Gideon said, very quietly, "We won't let anything happen to your children, Mrs. Benson."

She said suddenly, fiercely, "That's what you say, but who's to stop him? It isn't as if he'd have to do it himself; now he's out he could telephone someone down here, he's still got plenty of pals. As soon as you'd rung off this morning, I thought of that. That's why I didn't let them go back to school this afternoon. Mr. Gideon, how can you be sure he won't hurt my children?"

It had become an obsession.

Over the years, fear that her husband had been responsible for the Micklewrights' accident had been buried in her mind, and the message which Benson had sent back had quickened doubt to certainty. While he had been in jail she had felt safe; while he was out, she would live in a nightmare world of fear and dread, which would get stronger and more hideous as the days, perhaps as the hours, passed. Words wouldn't reassure her. The presence of the two policemen in the street wouldn't; in fact, nothing would, except her husband's recapture.

Gideon said, "I can imagine how you feel, but look at it straight for a minute. I'll have men outside this house day and night, until we get him. I'll double the present guard, too, and I'll make quite sure that—"

"You can't be sure," said Mrs. Benson flatly, and then went on deliberately: "Can you sit there and tell me to my face that you know he hasn't telephoned someone in London and told them what to do? Can you?

Gideon said, "Of course I can't."

"Well, there you are, then," Mrs. Benson said. "There's only one way . . ."

She broke off as the door burst open without warning. The way she jumped told Gideon just how keyed up she was, and how she must have fought to keep calm when he had first arrived. But no danger threatened. Instead, the twelve-year-old boy, young Syd Benson, came leaping into the room, with his sister behind him and only a little less excited. Gideon hadn't seen them for over three years. They looked nice kids: just anyone's children who were cared for properly and in good health, and who came from good-looking parents.

"Ma!" young Syd cried and skidded to a standstill in front of his mother. "You know what . . . ?"

"You'll get a slap round the side of your head if you don't go out faster than you came in," said Mrs. Benson. "I told you to stay and watch the television and not come unless I told you. Go on and do what you're told. Liz, I'm ashamed of you, you ought—"

"But Ma!" cried young Syd, standing his ground with a defiance which obviously wasn't unusual. "Dad's coming on television, it just said so on the news. *Had* to tell you that, didn't I?"

8 . The Reason for Fear

Young Syd's voice faded.

He looked into his mother's face, and showed his own shocked reaction to the way she took the news. She lost her color, and seemed to grow older in front of Gideon's eyes. It was only for a moment; then she braced herself, squaring her chin and her shoulders, and fought to throw off the crushing effect of what her son had said and—so much more important—how he had said it. Now, she looked down at him. He was small for his age; the girl was only an inch or two shorter. He was like Syd Benson; no one could mistake those sharp features, the rather thin lips, the chiseled look. And he had his father's light-blue eyes, with the unexpectedly long, dark lashes. He'd come bursting in to tell his mother that his dad was coming on the television; and in the way he had said it there was burning eagerness to see his father; excitement; welcome. The man whom his mother feared, whom she thought might harm these children, was this child's father; and the three years or more of separation hadn't altered that and hadn't altered the affection the boy felt.

Gideon found himself in the middle of a maelstrom of emotions, in depths which he only vaguely understood.

Then young Syd said, "He is, Ma, the announcer said so. Aren't you coming to see him? It's on . . ."

Mrs. Benson said, "Yes, Syd, I'll come. Will you come too, Mr. Gideon?"

"I'd like to," Gideon said.

"Well, hurry," urged young Syd.

He and his sister led the way. Ruby Benson looked once into Gideon's eyes, and then away; she was tight-lipped; and it was only possible to guess what was passing through her mind. Gideon followed her along a narrow passage to the long kitchen-cum-living-room, where the small-screen television set stood in one corner. It was dark outside, and there was no light on inside; the screen looked very bright. There were pictures of a speedboat undergoing trials on lakes which were probably in Scotland, and the loud roar of the engines throbbed about the room. The children took their seats; two larger chairs were placed so that any-one sitting in them could get a good view of the screen.

"Please sit down," Ruby Benson said.

They sat down.

"Do you know what?" young Syd burst out. "I haven't seen him for over three years!"

"Nor have I," piped up the girl, "and he's my dad, too."

Gideon heard Ruby Benson's sharp intake of breath. He saw that she was biting at her knuckles. There wasn't a thing he could do except sit there stolidly and watch and listen, understanding what was racking her. She hadn't said anything to try to turn them against their father; that was obvious. Right or wrong, she had let them have their own thoughts and memories of him, and now there was the excitement, this eagerness to see him; no sense of shame, no sense of fear.

The picture and the noise faded.

The male announcer came on.

"Now we take you for a brief visit to Millways jail, in the north of England, from which nine desperate criminals escaped this morning, three of whom have now been recaptured."

The announcer's face faded.

The high, gray, bleak walls of Millways jail were shown upon the screen, and there was silence except for the slight hum of the loud-speaker. The shots were done well, and the announcer did not spoil them with a running commentary; he let the prison speak for itself. The walls with the great curved spikes on the top; the small windows with the thick iron bars; the watchtowers; the shots from inside, with the galleries round the cells, the cell doors open, the convicts coming out, the great net spread between the galleries, to catch any prisoner who was fool enough to try to kill himself. Here was everything, with the warders, the gray-clad, gray-faced prisoners, the long rows of cells, the tiny holes in the doors, the inside of a cell with its bed, one chair, one small table, the pin-ups on the wall.

Everything.

The two children were absolutely still.

Gideon felt Mrs. Benson's hand touching his. He moved, so that he could take her hand, and felt the pressure of her fingers. She needed his presence, the warmth and stolidity of his touch, to help her now.

Then Liz spoke.

"I can't see Dad," she complained.

"You'll see him," the boy said. "Shut up."

The prison faded, and the announcer spoke from a screen filled suddenly with the one word: Wanted.

"We are about to throw onto the screen pictures of the six men who are still missing, and for whom the police in the whole of England are searching. By the side of the photographs will be a description which will help in the identification of the wanted men, each one of whom has a record of violence. . . ."

Ruby Benson said in a choky whisper:"They can't stay and see this, I ought to have stopped them, I—"

"Let them be," said Gideon, softly.

Neither of the children turned.

First, there was Jingo Smith, with his bald head and button of a nose, quite a merry-looking man; then, Wally Alderman, with his flat and broken nose, a man whom Lombroso would have welcomed as the perfect illustration of criminal type. Then, Matt Owens, small, with pointed features and one eye which twitched a great deal and, in the photograph, looked half-closed.

Then, Benson.

It was a good photograph; prison photographs were getting better. This showed him exactly as he was, and the boy staring at the screen might have been looking at himself as he would be in twenty years' time. Every line and every feature of Benson's face showed, and those thin lips.

Hair: Dark.
Complexion: Sallow.
Eyes: Pale blue.

That was what made his eyes so noticeable: clear, pale blue in a sallow face, the face that was almost olive-skinned.

Height: 5 ft. 9 in.
Distinguishing marks: Brown mole, left ear.
                            Appendectomy scar.
                            Tip of little finger of
                            left hand missing.

Then Benson was taken off.

Freddy Tisdale came on, looking almost cherubic, in spite of the starkness of the photograph. He gave the impression that he might burst into a smile at any moment. Ruby Benson stopped looking at the screen, but still sat there, as if hopeless. Gideon watched the children, and tried to imagine what was passing through their minds, but that was only for a moment. He leaned forward, took a brandy flask from his hip pocket, and unscrewed the cap.

"Have a sip," he said.

Ruby took it, blindly. When their hands touched again, hers were icy; she had gone cold in a few seconds. She choked a little, and Gideon took the flask away as the last picture faded and the screen went blank, then showed the announcer.

"Tomorrow, at the same time, WYN TELECASTING will

bring you up-to-the-minute news of events throughout the world. Now there will be an interval of . . ."

Gideon stood up. The children got up, too, and turned toward Gideon and their mother. It seemed very dark now that the screen was blank.

Quietly and steadily, young Syd's voice came.

"And you're the bloody copper who put him inside," he said. "What wouldn't I like to do to you!"

Gideon had built up the case against Benson.

Gideon had broken down Ruby's resistance, and had prevailed upon her to give evidence against her husband.

Now, Ruby heard her son speak like that.

This was a challenge which couldn't be set aside. If Gideon said nothing to the boy, then the hatred would only fester and there would be a new element: birth of contempt for the police. So Gideon had to take up the challenge, without hurting the mother too much, without showing the slightest sign of vengefulness. He had to make an impression which, later, might stand Sydney Benson's son in good stead.

"Come on, let's get out of here," young Syd said, and swung round toward the back door.

Ruby burst out, "Syd! Don't you dare!"

"I got to go where there's some clean air," young Syd sneered, and glowered at Gideon.

The girl stood there uncertainly, looking first at her mother and then at her brother, but never at Gideon. All Gideon did was to watch young Syd, catch his gaze and hold it. The boy tried to look away, but could not. They were more used to the dim light now.

Gideon said, "That's right, Syd, I did help to send your father to prison. But he knew the risk he was taking, and he knew for years that one day the police would catch up with him. They always do. Do you play football?"

Young Syd didn't answer.

Gideon said roughly, "You've got a tongue in your head, so answer me. Do you play football, or don't you?"

"I—yes. Yeh," repeated the boy, with a gulp.

"He's in the school team," Liz put in, as if glad to say something for her brother.

"Doesn't surprise me, he looks as if he's good at sports," Gideon said off-handedly. "All right, Syd, you're in the school team for football, but what happens when you foul one of the other side? The ref blows his whistle, and there's a free kick against you, isn't there? Do it in the worst place, the penalty area, and it's almost certainly a goal to the other side. What does that mean? If you break the rules, if you foul too often, you'll get kicked out of your school team. That's the way it works at school, and it's the way it works outside. We make certain rules. Most people obey them. Some think they can foul and get away with it. They do for a while; but sooner or later, they're found out. Your father didn't play to the rules. If he had, he'd be here with you today. It's as simple as that. I should have thought you would have known it by now, without having to ask a copper to tell you. Got it?"

The boy said, "Bloody copper, that's all you are," and he turned suddenly and ran swiftly toward the door which led to the scullery. In a moment, he was outside in the small yard; and as Gideon hurried after him, he heard the sound of his steel-tipped heels on the concrete of the yard. When Gideon reached the back door, young Syd Benson was climbing over the wall which led to an alleyway running between two rows of houses.

Behind Gideon was Ruby Benson, clutching the hand of her other child.

"Don't let him get away," she breathed, "anything could happen to him, don't let him get away."

The luck could run well, sometimes.

Gideon was outside and giving orders to Abbott and Old Percy, who came hurrying, when a police patrol car turned into Muskett Street. Radio messages flashed to other patrol cars, and in ten minutes young Syd was discovered with half a dozen other boys standing about an old warehouse not far from the Thames. Gideon didn't send a patrol car or a uniformed man to talk to the boy, but went himself. It gave young Syd a chance to show off in front of his pals, but it also gave Gideon an opportunity to find out if there was as much good in the boy as his mother hoped.

"Syd," he said, "you can play the game anyhow you like, but I've told you what will happen if you play it the wrong way. Now show some sense, and time it better. Fond of your mother, aren't you?"

Syd didn't answer.

Gideon swung round on another lad.

"Do you like your mother?" He flashed to a third. "And you? And what about you?"

He won a startled "Yes," an unexpected "She's okay," and a grunt.

"Been happy with your mother at home, haven't you?" Gideon asked young Syd, still roughly. "Come on, the others admit it, why don't you?"

"Ye-yeh."

"Well, she played to the rules, and she's made a man out of you," Gideon said, "If you hadn't a lot of guts you wouldn't have behaved like you did just now. But don't forget that your mother's having a tough time. I'm talking to you like this because I can tell you've got a good mind, and I won't insult you by pretending that you're just a kid who doesn't understand. You understand all right. Your mother's nervous because your father's out of jail; and if he comes and sees her, she'll want help, not hindrance. It's up to you to do all you can to help her, and pay back a bit of the debt you owe her. But if you don't want to, okay, I can't make you go back."

He was thinking, "If it comes to a point, I'll have to find some charge and pick the kid up; he'll be safer in a cell than out here tonight."

He turned and walked off, knowing that young Syd was being watched by Divisional men.

He went back to Muskett Street. There wasn't much that he could say, and he wasn't looking forward to the next interview; but he had another surprise. Ruby had controlled her fears and overcome the moment of crisis so well that she greeted him quite briskly.

"I shouldn't have let him watch, I suppose," she said, "but he'll soon come to his senses. The trouble is he mixes with the kids from Syd's old crowd, and there's nothing you can do about it. One of these days he's going to have to choose one way or the other, though I can't make him do it the way I want him to. The important thing is to make sure he doesn't run into trouble. You are having him watched, aren't you?" She was very anxious.

"Closely. He'll be all right, and I think he'll come back before long. We've got to decide what to do with him and the girl," Gideon went on. "I could arrange for them to go away somewhere; but if you send them now, you might make young Syd think that we're just trying to make sure that he can't see his father. That won't help on a long-term basis. Like us to put the girl somewhere, and leave you and young Syd here?"

There was a long silence. Then:

"We'd better all stick together," Mrs. Benson said.

Gideon went back to the Yard before going home.

Lemaitre had gone, and Sergeant Jefferson was there, holding the fort before a night-duty Chief Inspector came in; there was always someone in the Commander's office. Jefferson's gray head was bent over a report as the door opened, and he looked up quickly, then stood up.

"Didn't know whether you'd be looking in or phoning, sir."

"Best to look in," Gideon said. "Anything new?"

"Been very quiet, so far," said Jefferson. "Nothing fresh from Millways. That railway-sidings man who was beaten up is on the danger list. If he dies, that'll be a nasty job." Jefferson had a gentle way with him. "They've picked up a footprint near the Kelly's Bank vault, which might help; but in my opinion it's a bit tenuous, sir. Otherwise, just routine. I'm not expecting things to be so quiet tomorrow. Much warmer tonight, isn't it?"

Gideon smiled.

"We old-in-the-tooth coppers can tell the youngsters a thing or two, can't we? Well, I'm going home. Superintendent Fisher on duty tonight?"

"Yes, sir."

"Good. Pleasant dreams," said Gideon, and went off.

He looked in at the A.C.'s office and made sure that it was empty; had a word with Fisher, who had an office along the corridor; took a last look at the Information Room, studying recent teleprints from other parts of the country and the radio flashes. They were coming in fairly fast, he gathered; there had been five burglaries tonight so far, mostly on London's outskirts, nothing yet which the Divisions couldn't handle. He went off with a familiar feeling which was stronger at certain times than others, and was very strong now. It was a sense of anticlimax: a sense that when so much neded doing, he was walking away from it. The theme song of the Yard was unfinished business, and there was the guilty sense of going away at a time when anything might happen. The night held its secrets; perhaps the dead body, not yet discovered; or the killer, striking at this very moment. The burglar at the window or at the safe; the criminal at work everywhere; the never-ending cycle of the crimes committed by night and of the investigations beginning next morning.

He remembered, suddenly, that in the cell at H5 Division was a lad who might have taken the first steps on that long walk.

He, Gideon, was going home—to his wife, to supper and to bed.

Unless, of course, he was called out.

9 . Benson Alone

Benson did not know that his picture was being thrown onto the television screens all over the country. He stood in the kitchen of the furnished house, unable to hear the faint sounds from the radio in the next room, but hearing a louder, throbbing noise coming from the house next door; that was either radio or television, tuned too loudly. It got on his nerves. Everything was getting on his nerves, and he didn't realize that it was largely reaction to the fact that what he had planned so long and so carefully had actually gone according to plan.

Freddy Tisdale was out.

It was ten minutes to seven, and Freddy oughtn't to be long.

Benson began to wonder if he could trust Freddy.

Freddy had told him to stay here in the warm, there was no sense in their both going out; and that was right. It wasn't as if this job would be dangerous. It was five minutes' walk to the shop at the corner, and it would be child's play to get in, lift a few oddments of groceries, and get out again. Freddy, whose nerves seemed to be much steadier than Benson's that day, hadn't appeared to give it a second thought.

He'd been gone for twenty minutes.

Benson had opened the kitchen drawer and now stared at the knives, forks and spoons inside. His gaze was mostly concentrated on the knives. There was one, a poultry knife which had worn thin in the middle. It was very sharp. There was also a green felt sheath for a bread knife, to stop it from getting tarnished. He kept searching until he found a knife sharpener, took this to a tap and ran cold water on it, and then began to sharpen the poultry knife. Every now and again he paused, so that the grating hiss of steel on steel stopped, and he listened for the sound of Freddy's approach.

He heard nothing.

Freddy was to tap at the back door, three times.

Benson finished sharpening the knife, and drew the blade along his thumb; he just broke the surface of the epidermis. Then he slid the knife into the green felt sheath, tied it near the handle of the knife, and slid it all down the front of his trousers. He fastened the top of the sheath onto a trousers button, so that it would not work down, and then walked about, shifting the knife until it was in the most convenient position.

Now he was smiling.

He stopped smiling, for it was five past seven; Freddy had been gone a long time. He moved to the door, hesitated, put the light out, and then opened the door an inch. He could see the pale night, reflecting the snow. Some way off there were a few yellow lights, but not enough to worry him. He heard nothing.

Cold air swept in.

He closed the door and began to shiver, only partly from the cold.

Three things were possible.

One, that Freddy had been delayed, but would soon arrive with some food. With food.

Two, that he had deliberately run out on his partner.

Three, that he had been caught.

Benson didn't seriously consider the second possibility, but he had to consider the last. It made him sweat, in spite of the fit of shivering. He felt the gnawing at his stomach as if it were a sharp pain. Fear made it worse. He knew Freddy Tisdale only through prison life; he couldn't be sure that Freddy wouldn't break down and give a partner away. And the snow, which muffled all sound of approach, could muffle all sound of the police also, if they were coming.

Benson went upstairs, crept into an icy cold bedroom and, still shivering, moved to the window. He couldn't possibly be seen, yet he kept to one side, as if the night had eyes. He peered into the street, the white pavements and the banks of packed snow, the three neglected snowmen, the little houses with lights at the windows and at fanlights, all the front doors closed tightly against the bitter March wind.

He went back to the kitchen; and as he reached the door which led from the passage, he heard a dull sound. He stopped absolutely still, until it was repeated, and this time there was no mistake. *Bump, bump, bump.* This was Freddy; it must be. Yet, as he moved forward, Benson felt his heart almost choking him. Freddy might have been caught and might have given that signal away; he might open the door to a copper.

And Freddy might have returned—empty-handed.

Benson stood to one side, took the knife out and slid it into his trousers pocket, and then, left hand stretched out, he turned the key in the lock. Freddy could hear that. Then he opened the door a fraction of an inch.

"That you, Freddy?"

"Who the hell do you think it is?" Freddy demanded hoarsely. "Let me in, I'm frozen ruddy stiff."

Benson opened the door wider and Freddy came in, so cold that his teeth were chattering and his body shaking. His eyes looked sharply veined and glittery, his nose and his cheeks were blue, but he carried a cardboard carton, and the pockets of his stolen coat bulged.

Food!

Benson closed the door without a sound and switched on the light. He was breathing harshly, now. Freddy moved toward the kitchen table, dumped the box down, and then emptied his pockets; he didn't stop shivering.

"Flicking customers," he said, "there was a couple of women, standing there gassing; the shopkeeper and his perishing wife wouldn't let them go. I stood in a wind that cut like a flicking knife. Here, you dish up, I've got to go and get myself warm."

Benson didn't speak.

Steaming hot soup, ham, cheese, tinned potatoes, tinned peas, and some rye bread in a packet made a meal which might almost have come from the Savoy Grill. Benson and Tisdale hadn't eaten food like it for three years. They ate slowly and steadily for twenty minutes, until Freddy began to wilt. They had hardly uttered a word since his return.

Suddenly Benson said: "All we could do with is some beer. You got any beer?" He gave a tight-lipped grin.

"Like me to go and get some?" asked Freddy, also grinning. His face now had a much more amiable expression.

Benson said, "You're okay, Freddy, you've got what it takes. What are you going to do after we leave here? Stringing along with me or playing solo?"

"You any idea?" Freddy asked.

"We could play it both ways," Benson said. "I'm going

south, but let me tell you something. I've got a card index in my head, the best card index there is in the country. I know the name and address of every man and woman they think I might try to get in touch with, and I know the names of some people they won't even think about. I'm going to get in touch with some of those, and they'll do what I want them to do. They'll stake me, and they'll let me lie under cover. I don't need very long. I've got some dough put away, and I'm going to get out of this country just as soon as I've finished one little job."

"What's the job?"

Benson said, "Know who put me inside, Freddy?"

"No."

"My wife."

Freddy said, "Like hell she did! Nother guy?"

"I don't think she had one then, but that's one of the things I'm going to find out," said Benson. "There are a lot of things I'm going to find out." He fell silent for a moment, looking at Freddy through his eyelashes, those fine, dark, curly lashes which were reproduced in his son. "You know where you're going?"

"Syd," said Freddy Tisdale, in a quiet voice, "all I cared about was getting out of that place, and all I care about now is keeping out. I'd kill anyone who tried to stop me, and I mean it. And before I let them take me back, I'd kill myself. That's the way I feel about it."

"That's the way we feel about it," Benson said. "This is what we do. We keep together while we go down south; two can do that better than one, see. And I'll send you to a skirt who'll see you all right for as long as you need to lie low. When the heat's off, okay, we can get out of the country. We go it together until we get to London; that okay with you?"

"It's a privilege," Freddy said.

"That's what I like to hear. Now listen," Benson went on. "I don't want to play the luck too hard. We could stay here for three or four days, and then run right into trouble. I reckon we ought to leave here just before dawn in the morning so no one can see us, and then . . ."

Freddy said, "Syd, that would make me nervous. It'll be so cold then, and it's the wrong time of day anyway. Anyone who did see us would notice us, wouldn't they?"

Benson grinned.

"It's okay," he said, "you know the answers. Freddy, is there a big car park near here?"

"There's the one at the market."

"Market open tomorrow?"

"And every day."

"Could we get there around twelve o'clock, say, when the park'll be full, knock off a car, and get going?"

"We got to try something," Freddy said. "Why not that? If we leave here around half past eleven, anyone who sees us will think we've been looking over the house. That okay?"

"That's fine," said Benson. "Freddy!"

"Yeh?"

"You mean what you said about killing anyone who tries to get in your way?"

"I meant it."

"Okay," said Syd Benson. "So did I."

Next morning, Gideon woke up about seven o'clock, and lay for a few minutes looking at the sun shining in at a corner of the window. He heard no noises about the house; the only slight sound was of his wife's breathing, as she lay in the other bed. None of the children was about, then; the older they got, the later they were getting up in the morning. He eased himself up on his elbows; there was no break in his wife's even breathing. He got out of bed, shrugged on a dressing gown which made him look huge, pushed his feet into slippers, and went to the door. He'd bring her a cup of tea, as he often did. He glanced back at her from the door, and found himself smiling. She didn't look at her best, but she was all right; and when she was at her best she was really something. She wouldn't like the way her hair-net was half on and half off, but that didn't matter, either.

Gideon went out, and down the stairs.

This house at Hurlingham was not far from the Thames and the polo ground. The houses were in long terraces, each with two stories and an attic, and he had taken particular pride in his. Years ago, he had turned it from two flats into one house, and now the attic was set aside for the boys, including their sleeping cubicles; and the girls, Gideon, and Kate slept on the floor below. Gideon had done much of the converting himself and still kept the house decorated; if he had a hobby, it was woodwork and anything to do with painting and decorating. He liked to keep the value of his property up.

He had a good night.

Kate had been waiting for him, too, and he wasn't quite used to that. After the death of their son, seven years and more ago, they had gone through a very bad period, gradually growing apart and aloof from each other. At one time, Gideon had seriously wondered whether they would see their marriage through. Then, without quite knowing what had happened, things had changed.

There was no demonstration, but they began to understand each other again, and to enjoy each other's company. Gideon soon found this new atmosphere much, much better than he had ever hoped. It brought a sense of excitement even at home. It helped him to get more fun out of his children, too—their children now, rather than hers or his. The change was still sufficiently fresh for him to wonder at it; and to wonder, also, whether anything would happen to spoil it.

The truth was that he looked forward to coming home, and got home whenever he could. At one time, he had taken any excuse to stay at the office.

He made the tea, just for himself and ate; it was a rule that the children could have tea if they cared to make it for themselves—except on Sundays, when the girls were given a treat.

He thought he heard a tap running, upstairs, and then reached the landing and heard a door open.

Pru stood there in her peach-colored nightdress.

It was a funny thing, thought Gideon, but you saw your own daughter, day in and day out, from the time she was a toddler to the time when she was nearly twenty, and it took a moment like to make you realize that she was a young woman. Mary Rose hadn't a thing that his Prudence lacked. He hadn't realized that she had quite such a figure, her mother probably made her flatten herself a bit in her day clothes. Trust Kate.

Prudence looked young, fresh, pretty—and anxious.

"Dad," she said in a whisper, "what do you honestly think about Will Rose's chances?"

"If he didn't kill the girl, Pru, he'll be all right."

"Are you sure?"

"Positive."

"And you didn't mind Mary going to see you?"

"No, of course not." Gideon hesitated for a moment, and then looked at her very intently, suspecting something that she hadn't told him. "What's on your mind, Pru?"

"You really didn't mind?"

"Not a bit."

"Well, thank goodness," Pru said, "because there's something I didn't tell you. Yesterday morning, Mary rang me up, she was ever so upset, and she asked me if I'd have a word with you. I said it would be much better if she went to see you herself, and—well, you know what happened, don't you? I don't think she would have thought of coming to Scotland Yard if it hadn't been for me, and afterward I wondered if I'd rather let you down."

Gideon said, "You didn't let me down at all, Pru. Always fight for anything you believe in, and above all fight for your friends. Was she really a close friend?"

"Well, no. We did just know each other, but she's two years older than I, you see."

"You didn't know her well, then?"

"Not really."

"Like her?"

"Yes, everyone did."

"What kind of reputation did she have?"

"Dad," said Prudence, wisely, "I wish I knew what you were asking me all these questions for. What do you want to know?"

"Whether Mary Rose is a liar, Pru."

Pru didn't speak.

"Did she have a reputation as a liar?"

"No, everyone liked her."

"All right," said Gideon, "if she's telling the truth about what she and her brother did on Thursday, she'll be all right and so will he. If she's lying—well, it will do her more harm than good, and it certainly won't do him any good. Now you go and put a dressing gown on. I left a kettle on a low gas, if you want a cup of tea."

"Oh, thanks," said Prudence. "Thanks a lot, Dad."

Kate was awake, beginning to sit up, with the hair-net off and her hair unruly in an orderly fashion; she had pushed it together with her long, thin fingers. It wasn't really surprising that her daughters had good figures! Her eyes were bright, and she had something of Pru's freshness.

"Hear all that?" he asked.

"Yes," Kate said. "I only hope Mary Rose isn't lying."

Gideon got into the Wolseley a little after half past eight. Prudence wasn't going out until the afternoon, but would spend the morning practicing interminably on her fiddle. Penelope, their youngest girl, was still going to school, and had to go in the other direction. Priscilla, now sixteen, had just left school and had a job in a Chelsea office. Gideon dropped her off at the nearest corner to the office and watched her as she hurried, quite the young woman in her high heels and her nylons. She turned and waved, then disappeared. He grinned to himself, but there was a hint of a sigh as he started off again. Prudence first and now Priscilla had made him feel old. But that mood soon passed; and from then on until he reached the office, he was mulling over everything that had happened the previous day. The report was being prepared, as usual, and he grinned at the thought.

He wondered if any more of the escaped prisoners had been caught during the night.

None had.

There was only one change in the scene since yesterday; the quiet spell had ended, and in the Metropolitan area alone there had been forty-nine burglaries during the night, seven arrests had already been made. Fingerprints both at the Yard and at the Divisions were working to their limit.

There would be no time to spare today.

Lemaitre and Jefferson were in Gideon's office, and for twenty minutes they all went through the daily reports and made comments.

The three men from the Bond Street smash-and-grab raid would be up for the first magistrate's court hearing; in all, there were nineteen cases of major felonies up—most of them likely to be dealt with summarily, three likely to be sent for trial.

Lefty Bligh, the safe-breaker, had got himself a job as a messenger to a small firm of office consultants; and, by a strange coincidence, the office was on the same floor as a bookmaker's, where usually large sums in cash were kept in an ultramodern safe.

"Lefty will have a crack at that, soon," Gideon said. "Have two men always on the premises, to catch him red-handed."

"Right," said Lemaitre.

Next, Gideon glanced through the newspapers, which had difficulty in choosing between the Primrose Girl murder and the prison break. They solved their problems by sharing the space equally. There were photographs of six of the fugitive prisoners, including Benson; and there was a photograph of William Rose.

Before he started the usual briefing, Gideon looked through two medical reports which had been made about the accused boy. One was emphatic; he was perfectly sane and showed no indication of mental unbalance. The other, from a man whose name Gideon didn't know, suggested that there were indications of mental instability and recommended that the boy's medical history be carefully checked.

Gideon telephoned Smedd, who would have a copy of these.

"Yes, I'm getting a report from the boy's family doctor and his school doctor," Smedd said at once. "Should have them in today. I'll send you copies."

"Thanks very much," said Gideon. "Mind if I make a suggestion?"

"Very glad to hear it."

"Thanks. If there's a weakness in the case, it's the knife that was used. The boy could have lost it. Will you try to check, with the family, friends, people at his place of work, and make sure he didn't tell anyone else he'd lost it?"

"I'll see to that," said Smedd.

"Fine. Just as well to seal up all the holes," Gideon said, and felt that he'd done his duty by Prudence.

Next, he glanced through reports which were coming in fast from the Midlands and the North, saying that one or another of the escaped prisoners had been "seen." Such statements came from places hundreds of miles from Millways jail, and not one looked likely to stand up to scrutiny. Most of the provincial police H.Q.'s would be bombarded with these for days; and each would have to be checked. London's turn would come only too soon.

Then Gideon dealt with job upon job in the morning briefing, and by eleven o'clock most of the cases were off his desk. He felt that he could breathe again, and spent some of the next half hour checking in the protection plans for Ruby Benson and her youngsters; everything seemed to be in order, and there was a report that both children had gone to school that morning, escorted by two policemen who were waiting at the school to take them back.

"Keep a special eye on the boy," Gideon ordered. "He might cut and run for it."

"Yes, sir." It was Abbott who had reported, and who was still on duty in the street. "Any news of Benson, sir?"

"No," said Gideon, "and you keep a lookout, as if you're expecting him to turn into the street at any moment."

"Right, sir," said Abbott, in a tone which seemed to say: "If only he would!"

Gideon put the receiver down, and it rang almost at once; this time it was the A.C. He listened, scowled, and said, "I'll come along at once," but when he had put the receiver down again, he didn't move. Lemaitre looked up at him, one eye screwed up against the curling cigarette smoke, and asked, "What's that?"

"The P.P.'s still worried about Edmundsun."

"Why don't they learn to take our word for it?" Lemaitre was disgusted.

"They might have something," said Gideon; "and if they have, I'd rather find out what it is for myself, without being told. Oh, well, I'd better go along. Don't interrupt me unless it's about the Benson job."

"Right," said Lemaitre. "The papers have played it up pretty high, haven't they?"

"What else could we expect?" asked Gideon. "Benson's big news."

He spent twenty minutes with the A.C. and a senior official from the Public Prosecutor's office. The Edmundsun case weakness was worrying everyone, and one surprise defense witness, or the discrediting of a prosecution witness, could lose the case and set a known rogue free. But the talk got them nowhere, and Gideon went back to his office. Nothing important had come in, unless the newspaper which Lemaitre had spread over his desk was important. It was the *Evening Sentinel*, with a banner headline:

DID BENSON ESCAPE TO GET REVENGE?
POLICE WATCH ON FAMILY

"Here we go," Gideon said softly.

"Think he'll let himself be captured alive?" Lemaitre asked. "I should say . . ."

Gideon's telephone bell rang; and with that slow, deliberate movement, Gideon lifted it.

"Gideon."

"I've got Mrs. Benson on the line, sir," the operator said; "shall I put her through to you, or to Superintendent

Wrexall? He passed her call on to you yesterday, you may remember."

"Put her through," said Gideon quietly.

It was then exactly twelve o'clock on the second day of the escape.

10 . Twelve Noon

Gideon first heard Ruby Benson's agitated breathing, and guessed from that her frame of mind. It was just possible that she had heard from Benson; that she had received a sharper, closer threat. His job was to calm her down. He did not want to spend too much time with her, unless she had news of importance. Too much was pressing, and he had only two specific jobs: to make sure Benson didn't do her and the children any harm, and to catch Benson if he came down here. Easing Ruby's fear, soothing out the tensions which tormented her, were incidental; he mustn't spend too much time on it.

But he could help a bit.

"Hallo, Mrs. Benson, how are you this morning?" His deep voice had a comforting boom. "And the youngsters, they all right?"

"Yes, they—" Ruby broke off for a moment, and was breathing very hard. "Have you got him yet?"

"Not yet," Gideon said.

He hoped that by going to see her, he hadn't given her the impression that she could keep asking him for minute-to-minute news, and be continually on the telephone. The woman he had known in the past had realized the position, and been hesitant about taking his time, but now she was driven to desperation because of those fears for the children.

She said, "I know I shouldn't worry you, but I just don't know what to do for the best, Mr. Gideon. I didn't sleep much last night because of the worry of it, and this morning . . ." She broke off, almost choking.

"Well, what happened this morning?"

After a pause, she said hoarsely, "I'm sorry to behave like this, Mr. Gideon, but it was such a shock. I knew there was trouble for the children and me, but—well, there's a friend of mine at the shop where I work, I can't help it if you blame me for going about with him, but I've been on my own for so long and I had to—had to have some companionship. He's the manager at the shop, and this morning he had a—he had a phone call."

Gideon exclaimed, "From Benson?"—unbelievingly.

"No, not from Syd; he doesn't know who it came from," said Mrs. Benson quickly; "it was just someone who phoned up and asked for him, and—and then asked if he preferred lilies or roses. That's all, but—but it was the way he said it. And who else but Syd would send a message like that?" Her voice shook.

Gideon understood why much more clearly.

"It sounds like one of Benson's tricks," he agreed; "we always knew he had plenty of contacts in London. We'll keep an eye on your friend, Mrs. Benson. We've already got a man watching the shop, I'll have another to keep an eye on your friend—what's his name?"

"Arthur—I mean, Mr. Arthur Small."

"We'll keep an eye on him," Gideon promised. "Still feel that you'd rather have the children with you, or shall we find a safe spot for them until everything's over?"

She didn't answer at once.

One of the other telephones was ringing, and Lemaitre got up and came across to answer it, had a hand stretched out to pick up the receiver, and then heard a telephone ring on his own desk. He scowled as he picked up Gideon's.

"Mr. Gideon's on the other line, hold on." He went back, and was at his desk and speaking again before Ruby Benson answered Gideon.

"That's what's kept me awake all night, wondering what I really ought to do. I know it's silly, but I don't want to part with them now. I—I get a feeling that if I let them go I'd never see them again."

"You'll see them again," said Gideon, but knew that it was empty reassurance. "How's the boy?"

Another pause.

Lemaitre almost shouted into his instrument: "What's that?" and looked across at Gideon, his eyes blazing. "Hurry up!" he mouthed, and beckoned furiously.

Something big? Benson.

"Just a minute, Mrs. Benson," Gideon said, and clapped a great hand over the mouthpiece. "What's up, Lem?"

"Edmundsun," breathed Lemaitre; "got hold of a razor blade, tried to kill himself, they're rushing him to hospital. Might not live the day out, either. Who shall we send?"

"Cummings," said Gideon, without a moment's hesitation and put that out of his mind as he switched back to Benson's wife. "Sorry, Mrs. Benson. What were you saying?"

"You asked me how young Syd was," Ruby said, "and the truth is, I don't know. I knew he was interested in his Dad, I didn't think it was right to put him against his own father too much. To tell you the truth I always told myself young Syd would be a grown man and able to think for himself before he saw my husband again, and—but that isn't the point, Mr. Gideon! I don't know what to make of him. Seeing that prison on the television, and then seeing his father's photograph, did something to him. He seemed different last night, older if you know what I mean, as if—as if he'd been thinking, and wasn't so sure of me any more."

Gideon said, "Mrs. Benson, he's a healthy youngster, and he's got everything in him that he'll ever want. He'll pull through after this, you just needn't worry. Now, I must ring off."

"Yes, of course, I'm sorry I bothered you," Ruby said quickly. "Good-by, and—and thanks a lot."

"If you think we can help, any time, call on us," Gideon said. "Don't hesitate."

He rang off, and looked frowningly across at Lemaitre, who was briefing Cummings by telephone. One half of Gideon's mind listened to that. Lemaitre, who knew every trick in the book and every regulation that hampered or aided the Yard, could do this better than anyone else. If Edmundsun was really dangerously injured, Cummings must try to get a statement, but not offend the doctors. Cummings must also check with the Yard as often as he could.

Other things:

"Don't forget to have someone else as witness to any statement that Edmundsun makes. Don't forget to try to find out where Edmundsun salted the cash away . . ."

Throughout all this, Gideon kept seeing mind pictures of young Syd, who was so much like his father. Abbott was watching the boy, so he should be all right. But the problem was no longer a simple one of Syd's physical safety. It was possible to understand a boy worshiping a father whom he didn't know, a man whom his friends spoke of as a hero. It was impossible to foresee the consequences of such hero worship.

At twelve noon, the moment when Gideon was holding

on for Ruby Benson's call, Benson was closing the front door of the house where he and Freddy Tisdale had spent the night.

It wasn't so cold, but the snow was beginning to melt, and walking was difficult. Each of them, Tisdale in the lead, was well wrapped up in clothes found in the locked cupboards in the house; and each had a hat, Benson a bowler which was a little too big for him. Each had a muffler and gloves, too. They might have been exactly what they looked: a man from the estate agency with a prospective tenant who had been over the house. Two neighbors did, in fact, see them leave; neither gave them a second thought.

They walked on cautiously, because the ground was so slippery. At the corner, they could turn right toward a busy main road, or left, to a short cut toward the car park behind the market. Freddy turned left. They didn't speak, and their footsteps went *slsh, slsh, slsh*. Everyone on foot was intent on where he was stepping, and avoiding a nasty fall; no one took much notice of Benson and Tisdale. Every other man they saw was huddled up in clothes in much the same way, and no one was likely to single the fugitives out.

They had to cross another main road to reach the car park. They turned into it—and saw a sergeant of police leaning on his bicycle, talking to a constable. Both policemen were looking toward the corner, and both saw Benson and Tisdale.

Neither convict spoke or panicked.

Here was a testing time that was never likely to be repeated; they were on the same side of the road as the policemen, who stood close to a crossing. The road was busy. The only place to cross was near the policemen; anyone who tried to cross this side of them would invite attention. The two men had turned toward the policemen, and couldn't turn the other way without attracting attention, either.

They walked on.

They still watched the ground, picking their steps carefully. Here, outside the little shops, the snow had been cleared in most places, but there were slushy patches, and walking wasn't wholly safe. Benson, three yards from the policemen, actually glanced up and looked straight along the road, while Tisdale glanced toward the other side.

The sergeant wasn't looking at them, now.

The constable was.

Benson's whole body seemed to be screaming. Every muscle was ready, to move, to take him across the road, to go tearing toward the car park, but he knew that if he were recognized he would never get away. He sensed that Freddy suffered from exactly the same screaming tension.

Twenty yards away, a child stepped off the curb.

The mother cried out, a cyclist jammed on brakes which squealed, a motorist hooted. Policemen and sergeant looked round, abruptly, and Benson and Tisdale reached the crossing. They had to wait for two cars. Even when these passed, they didn't hurry. They were breathing into the thick woolen mufflers, and looking out of the corner of their eyes toward the men in uniform, one of whom was moving toward the woman and the child.

Benson started across the road.

They reached the other side.

Neither said a word as they slipped down a narrow alley toward the car park. Here, the thaw didn't seem to have been so rapid, and the snow was much harder. A boy came running toward them, making a slide, and Benson moved to one side. The boy was about young Syd's age, wrapped in a red muffler and wearing a school cap, his eyes a clear blue and his plump cheeks a bright red.

The two men reached the car park.

It stretched a long way in each direction, and beyond it were the canvas-covered stalls of the big market. There must have been three hundred cars in all, side by side, parked as closely as an expert parking attendant could put them. The ground sloped a little in one direction, and there were two big arrows with the words: WAY OUT.

Few people were about.

"One near the exit," Benson said. "Try the doors as we pass."

"Yeh."

The snow was crunchier here, too, because fewer people had walked on it. They passed between two lines of cars. Not far off, an engine started up and a car moved toward the exit, its exhaust fumes thick and smelly. Freddy paused at the back of a small car which had a front window down, and stepped between it and a green Jaguar. The small car's driving door wasn't locked, either.

"This'll do," he called.

"Okay," said Benson.

He slid between the car and an Austin Seven which was parked on the other side. He had difficulty in squeezing in, for there was so little room to spare, but he managed. Freddy was already working at the ignition with a piece of wire he had brought from the house. His hand looked cold, although he had been wearing gloves, and he couldn't get the "key" to work. He began to swear under his breath. Benson watched him, but looked into the driving mirror, and saw a big, fattish man coming toward him—toward this line of cars. The newcomer was talking to someone behind him, for Benson could see his lips moving.

A small, wizened man appeared by the big man's side. Benson drew in a sharp, hissing breath.

"What's up?" Freddy asked sharply.

"Get it started!"

"Give us a chance. What . . ."

Benson drew in another hiss of breath. Freddy glanced up, saw the tension on his companion's face and the way he watched the driving mirror. Freddy couldn't see anyone in it, from where he was sitting, so turned his head round. He saw the big man going along the line of cars, and the little, wizened man coming toward them.

It was the car park attendant.

Benson had seen the man's face clearly; the gray stubble, the slobbery lips, one eye which watered badly. He had seen the cap, the woolen muffler tight round the thin neck, the bundle of coats he was wearing, and the ticket machine and leather cashbag which was strapped to his waist.

Freddy said urgently, "What's he after?"

Benson said softly, "It's Taffy Jones."

Freddy's breath hissed, as if Benson had said: "It's the Millways Governor." Until a year ago Jones had been in Millways, a prisoner serving a short-term sentence. He should have had ten years, but had squealed on three men who had done a job with him, so he'd got off lightly. He would always squeal; he was a man whom it was impossible for these two to trust.

And he could not fail to recognize them.

He had reached the back of the car, and was pushing his way toward them, the chinking money in the worn leather bag, the bright metal ticket dispenser shining. There seemed to be no particular animosity on his face as he reached the window near Benson, bent down, and looked in. The window was open several inches at the top.

Then, his mouth gaped. His broken teeth showed. He stood like that, half-crouching, hemmed in by the car behind him, one hand at the window, and the other out of sight. His watery eyes, the one half-closed, held an expression of shocked horror. There was no shadow of doubt that he had recognized them.

And he was a squealer.

There was a split second in which none of them moved. Then, two things happened at once: the ignition light on the dashboard panel showed, as the home-made key made contact; and Benson dropped one hand to his pocket, the other to the door handle, the window shot down.

Taffy Jones gave a gurgling kind of cry, and turned, and started to run. The fat man's car started up, drowning the sounds. There was so little room, and the slush running beneath his feet was ankle-deep. He skidded, gave that gasping cry again, and crashed down, slopping into the slush, splashing the cars, splashing Benson as Benson slid out of the seat. Freddy was out of the other door, almost as swiftly, and he looked right and left, but saw no one. Now, Jones was writhing and squealing, and trying to get to his feet, but he had very little time; and the fat man's car was noisy as it moved off. Jones twisted his head round. He looked like a cretin as he did that; the expression in his eyes and the slobbering saliva at his mouth were revolting.

"I woan talk, I woan talk, I woan talk," he moaned. "Doan 'urt me, I woan talk . . ."

Benson skidded, regained his balance, went down on one knee beside the man—and the poultry knife was in his hand. He had used a knife before, expertly. He used it now. It slid through the thick coats, the shirt, the skin, the flesh. It went straight to the heart, and Taffy Jones' moaning and writhing stopped, there was just the rattle in his throat, strangely subdued, and then a quivering into stillness.

Freddy appeared.

"Got to get rid of him quick," he said, "but put his bag in the car, come in useful that will."

11 . Deep Snow

Benson was getting to his feet, slowly, and wiping the knife on the dead man's coat. He didn't speak. Except that his lips were set more tightly than usual, there was nothing different about him. He bent down, and used the knife to slash at the leather strap which held the moneybag to the dead man's side. He picked the bag up, and the coins jingled; a sixpence fell out and dropped, to bury itself in the snow. Benson fastened the flap, and pushed the bag through the open window. Now, he looked about him, and Freddy Tisdale did the same; but no one was in sight, although in the distance two cars started up, and that meant that they would soon be passing the end of this row.

Benson said, "Didn't I see a car with a plastic cover over it?"

"Little one, left side row."

"Let's push him under."

"Okay," said Freddy. "Can you lift him?"

"Yeh."

"I'll keep a lookout," the younger man said.

When on tiptoe, he could see all over the car park, and to the moving cars which were converging toward the exit from different directions. Neither of them would come near, but either driver might glance their way.

Benson was picking up the dead man.

"Hold it," Freddy said.

Benson stood upright, and might have been carrying an empty sack, for all the strain his face showed; but he felt something wet on his hand. He watched Freddy tensely, until the cars passed and Freddy said:

"Okay now."

Benson moved swiftly, with Freddy leading the way. Freddy reached the little car, finding that the aluminum-colored plastic sheet over it was laden with snow which was beginning to thaw. It was tied to each wheel with tapes. Freddy could have cut these; he didn't, but plucked at one corner with his cold fingers until the knot gave away. He pulled the tapes out and lifted the plastic, but it caught against the running board; this car was twenty years old if it was a day. He eased the plastic up, and then

78

Benson put Taffy flat on the ground by the side of the car, and shoved him underneath, pushing first with his hands and then with his feet. As soon as the body was completely hidden, Freddy tied the corner back again.

But the melting snow was stained with crimson.

Neither man spoke, but each scooped snow off the top of the plastic cover, and dropped it on to the blood, concealing it. Then they went back the way Benson had come, scuffling up snow with their feet to cover the bright red drops. They got back to the car, and the red ignition light still glowed. Freddy pressed the self-starter. It whined. He pressed again, and it whined more shrilly.

"Cold as ruddy charity," he said, and pressed again. The grating, whining sound seemed to echo all over the great park. A car which they hadn't heard start up moved toward the exit, followed by two more. Freddy peered through the windscreen and, in the distance, saw a little group of men; it looked as if something had happened to make them all come into the park together.

"Get it going," rasped Benson.

Freddy was sweating.

"Hold your ruddy trap!"

Benson opened his mouth, but didn't speak. Freddy tried again, and there was just the grating, metallic sound, setting their teeth on edge. The other men were drawing much nearer. Benson could now see them, and he had a hand on the door handle and another in his pocket.

The engine spluttered.

"Got—" began Freddy, and it died again. He began to swear at it in a low-pitched voice, and he didn't stop even when the engine stuttered again, then began to turn more freely. He pressed the accelerator gently at first, to woo a welcome roaring. The car quivered. Freddy eased off the brake and moved slowly forward. He didn't say, and Benson didn't say, that the great fear now was that the car belonged to one of the men heading their way.

They got out into the lane leading toward the exit, and in the driving mirror Freddy saw at least six men, talking and chatting. No one shouted. Freddy went up a gear, approached the roadway and turned toward the wide exit. Beyond was a street with a timber yard on one side and a small factory opposite. A timber truck was backing out, and a man behind it was holding up the approaching traffic, including Freddy. Freddy flicked the gears into neutral and waited while the great truck swung round in

front of him. Benson did not glance at him. Three cars
came in quick succession from the car park, one moving
very fast. Freddy saw this leaping upon them in the
mirror, and his sudden, hissing breathing made Benson
look round. The car behind pulled up, brakes groaning;
but neither man inside got out, just waited patiently.

"Okay," Benson said.

Ten minutes later they were out of the built-up area,
and driving along a main road leading south. The road
itself had been cleared, but banks of snow on either side
were huge and massive; water from them, thawing out,
was running across the road; the wheels kept splashing
through it.

Benson turned round, leaned over the back of his seat
and picked up the cashbag. He took out a handful of
small silver, mostly sixpences, and began to count. It took
a long time. "Twenty," he would say. "Ten bob"—and
drop that money into one pocket. Again: "Twenty—that's
a quid." "Twenty—thirty bob." Then after a few minutes,
there was a note of deeper satisfaction. "Some two bobs
and half-dollars in this pocket, 'bout time too."

The counting took him twenty minutes.

"Talk about a day out," he said; "that's five quid all
but two bob."

"I'll take the odd money," Freddy grinned.

"Like hell you will. How's the petrol?"

"Half empty."

"Why don't you be an optimist and call it half full?
Okay. We drive on for a couple of hours and then we'll
make a change. I want to make a phone call, too."

After a long pause, Freddy asked:

"Who to?"

"Pal o' mine," said Benson, and now he was smiling.
"Pal I can rely on, too. Knows my so-called wife. Sent
me up a message by Jingo's wife a coupla times. Know
what? My wife's got a boy friend, a sissy who runs a
dress shop! How do you like that? Nice-looking *gentleman*, I'm told."

The car went speeding on. No one took any notice of
them from the roadside. More powerful cars flashed by
them, splashing the melting snow onto the windscreen.
The sun was breaking through reluctant cloud, and it was
warmer than it had been for three weeks.

"You going to put that right?" Freddy asked.

"I'm going to put a lot of things right," said Benson.

"They can only put me back again. Freddy, you take a tip from me. You do everything you want to do, while you can. They'll pick us up for the car park job unless we can get out of this flicking country; and if we get out, it's got to be soon." He paused, but soon went on: "I know a man who can fix it for the pair of us. He'll want five hundred nicker—how much can you put your hands on?"

"I dunno," Freddy said; "but if I need five hundred nicker to get my head out of a flicking noose, I'll find it. This chap okay?"

"Yeh."

"There's only one thing we can do," Freddy Tisdale said, "we can try, can't we? I wouldn't like to be the guy who meets me and recognizes me. No, sir!"

He laughed on a high-pitched note.

Then: "We could stop for some fags," he said. "And I wouldn't mind a cuppa."

"We go on until we're ready to ditch this car," said Benson, emphatically. "We want to be within walking distance of a town when we do that, too."

"We want to be in a town," Freddy said, very thoughtfully. "We want to leave this wagon in a car park or some place where no one will think it looks funny. We aren't so far from Stoke. That be okay?"

"That'll be okay," Benson said.

That was at a quarter past one.

At a quarter past two, held up by traffic and by some roads partly blocked by snow, they reached Stoke. They left the car in a crowded car park, shared the money, and walked off together; no one took any notice of them. They had ham sandwiches at a snack bar, keeping their hats on like several of the other people, and finished up with sweet, strong tea. They bought cigarettes and chocolates, and then went out of the café. Walking about in the town, among people dressed in ordinary clothes, was like a dream. They kept together, didn't talk much, and looked like two reasonably prosperous businessmen. Benson's shoes began to pinch, but he didn't complain.

At half past three, he went into a telephone booth, and Freddy watched him from the outside. He put a call through to a Mile End number, then waited, leaning against the side of the booth and watching Freddy and the passersby.

A man came up and obviously wanted to use the telephone. He hung about.

Noises on the line.

A girl operator's sharp voice: "You're through, caller."

Benson said, "That you, Charlie?" He paused just long enough for the man to say yes, and then went on: "Listen, Charlie, I'm coming down to see you, be there in a couple days. Had an unexpected holiday, see. Bit o' luck, wasn't it?"

Charlie said with a gasp, "Yes, yes—it—listen. Be—"

"It's okay," Benson said, "I'm going to be careful. But do something for me, Charlie. I want to see my kid. You know. The boyo. They're keeping a pretty sharp eye on him, aren't they?"

"You couldn't say a truer word," Charlie told him, and then waited, breathing noisily into the telephone.

"Well, get him away from them," Benson said. "He'll be anxious to see his dad, won't he?" Even Freddy, watching his companion's face, realized that Benson's smile was as evil as a smile could be. "Just have him there for me, Charlie, and don't go making any mistakes, you know what could happen if I were to open my trap. Oh, and Charlie?"

"What?"

"Don't forget what I could tell the world about you," Benson said. "Expect me when you see me, old cock. So long."

He rang off.

The man who had waited to use the telephone was staring impatiently. Benson kept his face covered, and the man went straight into the telephone booth and dropped pennies into the box. Benson and Freddy walked off briskly, with danger forever on their heels.

"We going to knock off another car?" Freddy asked.

Benson said, "I don't want to play my luck too far. We want a car that no one will miss until morning, and the way to fix that is lay up in a house until after dark, then take a car out of a garage. Say we pick another empty house, and keep an eye on our neighbors. That okay?"

"Sure," said Freddy.

Twenty minutes later, they found the house they were looking for. They also saw the house, across the road, from which they could probably take a car. At the moment the car wasn't there; but the garage was standing empty, doors wide open. A young woman, quite something to look at, could be seen moving about inside the house, often a silhouette against the light which she had put on early.

Freddy Tisdale couldn't keep his eyes off her.

Soon, it was dark.

The husband came home in a small car, which he drove straight into the garage. The young woman hurried out, and neither man nor wife realized that they were being watched.

"They haven't been married long," Benson said, grinning. "Looks okay."

"Looks wonderful to me," Freddy said. "Maybe I'll give her a nice surprise, and stay the night."

For Gideon, the rest of that day was wholly unsatisfactory. Days came like it every week, sometimes two or three times a week, but there was seldom the degree of urgency and gravity which he sensed now. There was no news at all about the six men from Millways, except the reports, which were coming from a wider area than ever, that one or the other of them had been seen. The Yard, the London Divisions, the Home Counties, the Midlands and the North country police stations were swamped with such reports, and dozens of men were being interviewed; none was really like any one of the wanted men.

Gideon knew nothing of the body under the car in the car park.

He knew nothing of the furnished house or the burgled grocery shop.

He knew nothing about the two men in the empty house opposite No. 24 Wittering Street, Stoke-on-Trent.

The police just weren't getting the breaks. The evening newspapers were adopting a sharper note, there were two editorials about slackness at Millways jail, and with six prisoners still at liberty there was likely to be a lot of public anxiety. Gideon knew how often these things ran in cycles. Once a moan started, there would be the risk of a barrage of complaints, and with the perverseness of fate, or whatever directed the affairs of men, there would probably be a run of poor results. Already, there was Edmundsun's suicide in the remand cell at Brixton to make ammunition for the critics.

It was all very well to shrug one's shoulders and pretend

to ignore or be indifferent to these periodic attempts to ginger-up the Force, but they got under one's skin, and could make the difference between doing a good job and a bad one. Gideon wasn't absolutely proof against them, Lemaitre certainly wasn't, and young chaps like Abbott probably keyed themselves up until they were almost nervous. People too easily forgot that policemen were human.

Edmundsun had died without making a statement. He had probably had accomplices in the embezzlement of nearly forty thousand pounds from a big commercial banking house; and for Cummings and the Fraud Squad there was likely to be week after week of slow, laborious research to try to recover the missing money and to find out who had conspired with the dead man.

The evening papers headlined the suicide and the fact that the six escaped prisoners were still at large. Two of them came out with stories about Ruby Benson's fear, and of the police watch on her and the children.

Gideon had at least made sure that everything was moving as it should. In a quiet way, the Yard had geared itself to exceptional efforts, since five of the six men still at liberty were Londoners. Their wives, their homes, their friends, their children, were all kept under surveillance. There was no way to hide the fact that this was being done; and Gideon had the sinking feeling that Benson, at least, would be smart enough not to come home. But one couldn't tell. He might act on the belief that Muskett Street would be the last place the police would expect him to go. Or he might be driven by desperation, hunger, and cold. These factors were more likely to lead to the recapture of the men than anything else.

The police could usually sit back and wait.

They couldn't afford to, with men like Benson and the others.

It was nearly seven o'clock when Gideon checked everything, yawned, saw patient, gray-haired Jefferson making out reports, and then stood up, fastening his collar and tie as he did so.

"I'm off, Jeff."

"Good night, sir."

"Call me if there's anything worth while; I'll be home all the evening."

"I'll try not to worry you, sir."

"I'll be in the sergeants' room for the next ten minutes," said Gideon. He put on his big hat and went out, letting the door close behind him on its hissing hydraulic fixture. The rubber tips at his heels made little sound as he moved along the bare, brightly lit corridors. Two or three junior men passed him. He went up one flight of stairs, and then into the big room where he expected to find Abbott and probably Cummings. Yes, they were there, sitting together at a table, probably exchanging notes.

They stood up at Gideon's approach.

"Sit down," he said, and ignored the other sergeants in the room. "Thought I'd catch you here. How'd things go, Abbott?"

"Absolutely uneventful, sir," said Abbott. "I had a word with the Divisional Inspector who came round just before I was off duty. He says there's nothing at all to report, none of Benson's known friends have heard from him."

"Known friends" was good.

"It's the beggars we don't know about that we're after," Gideon said. "Anything else?"

"Benson's wife looks pretty worried, sir, and there's the man Small—he went to her home tonight. I gather he's going to stay there until it's all over. He looks a bit edgy, too."

"Who wouldn't? The children?"

"The girl clings to her mother. As for that boy—well, sir," said Abbott, with obvious feeling, "I don't know him well enough to be sure, but he looks as if he could turn out to be a nasty customer. He didn't actually say anything to me, but . . ."

Gideon smiled. "Looks could kill, eh? Yes, he might be strongly pro-Dad. Watch him closely."

"I will, sir!"

Gideon concealed his smile, then; the eagerness of a new man always struck him as amusing; pleasing, too. He turned to Cummings, who wasn't so young—in the middle thirties, in fact. It was a pity how Cummings ran to fat; he looked flabby and startlingly pale against Abbott's healthy tan. His gray eyes always had a rather tired look, in spite of his needle-sharp mind. It was hard to believe that he had a genius for figures and could find his way through involved books of accounts which were Greek to Gideon.

"No luck at all with Edmundsun, eh?" Gideon said.

"I was by his side from the minute I reached the hospital, but couldn't get a word," said Cummings. "Just muttered his wife's name once or twice before he died, that's all."

"Any ideas who did the job with him?"

Cummings didn't speak.

"Well?"

"Don't like guessing," said Cummings, winning Gideon's silent applause, "but you know that Mr. Harrison and I were always worried about the chief prosecution witness—the manager of Edmundsun's department, furniture and household hire purchase. Now I come to think of it, it wouldn't surprise me if the manager isn't deliberately being obscure. He's no fool. Used to be a solicitor, and he knows a lot of the tricks. If he worked on the job with Edmundsun, he may have planned to give his evidence so as to get Edmundsun off. It's only a guess, sir, but it could be worth following up."

"What do you think of the chap? Man named Elliot, isn't it?"

"Yes. And he's all right as a person, sir, affable as they come. But that's nothing to go by."

"No, it isn't," Gideon agreed. "Well, I'm going to arrange for you and probably a couple of others to concentrate on the job; I don't like the idea that anyone might get away with forty thousand quid." He scratched his chin, and the stubble rasped. "Edmundsun kept calling his wife, you say. She get there in time?"

"Ten minutes late."

"How'd she take it?"

"Well, pretty calm, as a matter of fact."

"Know what I'd do," said Gideon, thoughtfully; "I'd have a word with her as soon as possible. Don't put anything into plain language; but just make it clear you're sure that someone else was on this job with her husband, and that, if it wasn't for them, he'd be alive today. If she knows anything, that might persuade her to talk. Worth trying, anyhow."

"I'll fix it first thing in the morning," Cummings promised.

Gideon knew that he would.

There was no garage at Gideon's house, and he left his car at a garage nearby, then strolled toward his house, along the dimly lit street. The weather had changed with a vengeance, and he was almost too warm with his heavy topcoat and his woolen waistcoat. As he neared the house, he thought he saw someone lurking in the shadows of the doorway, and, with a caution learned over the years, he slowed down and approached carefully.

Then he grinned.

They were lurking figures all right, boy and girl. Prudence and a lad. Kissing. Gideon coughed loudly, saw them spring apart, saw Prudence look at him in confusion, and the youngster stand stiffly, almost to attention.

"Mind you two don't catch cold," Gideon said. "Hallo, Pru. Hallo, young man."

"Good evening, sir!"

"Oh, Dad, this is Raymond . . ."

Kate was alone in the kitchen; one of the boys still living at home was out, one upstairs in the attic playing with his electric train set. The two younger girls were out, too, one of them at night school, one with friends. Kate, in a royal blue dress, looked fresh and handsome and obviously pleased to see him. That did him a lot of good. Funny, to find the old affection warming up again. They weren't demonstrative and didn't kiss.

"Did you know about Raymond?" asked Gideon.

Kate smiled. "They don't stay young forever," she said, "and now Pru's finished her exams she'll have more time for boys." Then, obviously because she thought of the Primrose Girl and the boy in the police station cell, her smile faded. "Any news?" she asked.

"No change," said Gideon.

That was at half past eight.

Just after nine, the telephone bell rang; and Priscilla, the middle daughter, as fair as Prudence was dark, went hurrying to answer it. Gideon caught Kate's eyes, and realized what she was hinting: that Priscilla was showing remarkable eagerness to answer the telephone.

He raised his hands, helplessly.

"They grow up too fast for me," he said ruefully, and looked round at the door which Priscilla had left open. He heard her eager voice, and then the flat disappointment which came into it.

"Yes, he's in," she said, and called: "Dad! It's Sergeant Jefferson, wants to speak to you."

Gideon, coat off, collar and tie loose and shoelaces undone, got out of his big armchair reluctantly, and strolled toward the little room where the telephone was.

"Hallo, Jeff," he said.

"Thought you'd want to know this, sir," said Jefferson. "Two more of the Millways chaps caught—Alderman and Hooky Jenkins. They were in a Manchester railway yard, they'd traveled on a freight train. Almost certain that they killed that railwayman. Manchester rang through to say they'll do everything they can to find out if this pair knows which way the others went, sir."

"That's fine," said Gideon, quietly. "Thanks for calling, Jeff."

Now there were four, including the worst of them.

He wondered where Benson was.

Soon afterward, Gideon went to bed. That coincided, although he could not have the faintest idea of the coincidence, with the first offensive move of that persistent thief, Lefty Bligh, and a younger man whom he was training in the gentle art of cracking a crib without making too much noise. Lefty used an oxy-acetylene cutter of a special miniature design. They went across to the bookmaker's door, with a fortune inside waiting for the taking.

His companion watched and marveled at the ease with which Lefty got the door open, dismantled the burglar alarm, and made the whole process look child's play. Both Lefty and his apprentice went boldly inside.

A light came on.

"Hallo, Lefty," a Yard detective-sergeant greeted. "Want something?"

Lefty was one of those criminals who did not believe in violence. He looked as if he could cry. His apprentice made a run for it, but was met at the lift by another Yard man, and promptly gave up trying.

12 . Farther South

About that time, too, Benson was staring across at the house where the young couple lived.

He was sitting on a box close to the window of the house where he and Tisdale had taken refuge. It wasn't furnished, and there was no comfort, but the night was much warmer, and they weren't really cold. They'd eaten two hours before, and had enough food left for another day. They'd sat here, watching the couple sitting by the side of a fire in the house opposite, eating supper from a tray. The more they saw, the more they realized that these were newlyweds; the man couldn't leave the girl alone, and she didn't exactly look as if she resented it. They'd gone toward the door, about twenty minutes ago, their arms round each other; then they'd put out the downstairs light. Now, there was a light on in the upstairs front room, and Freddy was actually licking his lips.

The girl appeared near the window.

"What the butler saw," Freddy muttered; "what wouldn't I give for a chance to change places with him?" Freddy sounded as if he wasn't feeling so good. "How about it?"

Benson said, "You've waited three years, you can wait another few days. We stay here until they're asleep, and then we go and get the car. We push it out of the garage and down the road."

"Okay," Freddy said. "I hope we don't disturb their dreams."

Soon, the girl came and stood at the window, with her face in shadow. The man joined her. Suddenly, the girl stretched up and drew the curtains; she made quite a picture. Freddy swore beneath his breath, and watched shadows.

It was twenty minutes before the light went out.

It was another half hour, and nearly half past eleven, when Benson and Freddy left the empty house. They crept into the deserted street. Except for the odd late bird, no one was likely to be about tonight; everyone who had been to the pictures was home. Only two windows in the whole street showed a light, and there was no parked car.

They crossed the road to the silent house.

The drive, made of smooth cement, sloped slightly upward toward the garage. They made no sound as they reached it. Freddy examined the lock and saw that it was just a padlock with a hasp; elementary. He took out a small screwdriver which he had brought from the furnished house, and set to work on it.

Benson watched the upstairs window and the street.

There was no sound.

Only a few street lamps, at intervals of fifty yards or

more, gave any light, and suddenly these began to go out, one by one. The sound of metal on metal sounded very loud. Then, the padlock opened and Freddy whispered,

"We're okay."

But when they opened the garage doors, one squeaked alarmingly. Both men stood stock-still, watching the upstairs room.

Janice Morency, a bride of only three weeks, felt the snug warmth of her husband beside her and heard his steady, rhythmic breathing. She was just beginning to learn how quickly he could drop off; he would be wide awake one moment, glorying, and fast asleep the next. The house was very quiet. The street was quiet, too.

The glow from the street lamps began to go out, as they always did at half past eleven.

Then Janice heard the garage door squeak.

She went absolutely rigid with alarm, for she knew the sound so well. She heard it every morning when Frank opened the gates, heard it every time she moved the door herself; there couldn't be any mistake at all.

"Frank," she whispered, "wake up. *Frank!*"

For a tense moment after the door had creaked, Benson and Freddy Tisdale were as still and silent as the girl. Then Benson whispered, "Okay, get inside."

"Suppose . . ."

"Inside, close the doors!"

"But supposing they come . . ."

"And supposing they don't," Benson said flatly.

There was just room for them to squeeze into the garage and pull the door to; it didn't squeak when being closed, only when being opened. They stood in the near darkness. There was a window, which showed just a glim of light, and they worked their way round toward it, then stared up at the house. Benson could tell that Tisdale was more on edge than he had been at any time; some people were at their worst late at night. He didn't watch Tisdale, only the house. If a light went on . . .

Freddy said uneasily, "We could be trapped in here."

"If anyone comes down to see if the door's open, we know what to do," Benson said. "We can't lock the door again; if he comes down he'll find the door open, and he'll raise the alarm anyway. Right?"

Freddy muttered, "I suppose so."

Then the light went on in the front bedroom of the house.

They could just see the window from their point of vantage, and they saw the bright light shine out. A moment later, the light got brighter; that was because the curtains were pulled back. There were shadows; and then suddenly the head of a man appeared, turned toward the garage. He could see the doors from here, but couldn't tell whether they were locked.

Could he?

Benson stood quite still, his right hand touching the poultry knife.

Frank Morency, tousled head and broad shoulders out of the window, and his wife pressing close against him at one side, saw nothing but the outline of the garage, the roof of the house next door, the gardens in the street, the dark road and slender lampposts. He shivered as wind cut along from the east, and backed inside.

"You must have been dreaming," he said.

"Frank, I swear I wasn't."

"Well, have a look for yourself," he suggested, "but go and put a dressing gown on, I don't like you appearing in public like that."

He was laughing at her!

"But I heard the sound, I've heard it so often!"

"All right, look for yourself, but—" Morency stopped abruptly when he saw the change in his bride's expression, slid an arm round her, squeezed, and then said, "Like me to go down and have a look round, sweetheart?"

She didn't answer.

"I will, like a shot," he said.

"If you're sure the doors are still shut . . ."

"I'm positive!"

"Then I suppose I must have dreamed it," Janice said.

She didn't really believe that; she was sure that she had heard a sound, but no longer sure that it had been the garage door. They went back to bed, where for a few minutes the warmth and the strength of his body comforted and reassured her; then he began to breathe very smoothly and rhythmically again, and for the first time in her married life she felt a kind of loneliness.

Soon she dozed off.

Freddy Tisdale stood back from the hinges of the garage doors, an oilcan in his hand, thin oil smearing his fingers. He was breathing very softly, and keenly aware of Benson's watching eyes. The bedroom light had been out for half an hour, and the street seemed absolutely deserted.

"Try it now," he said.

"Okay." Benson began to push the offending door, cautiously. When halfway open, it gave a faint squeak, but nothing like the noise it had made before. This time, no light came on.

Soon they were wheeling the car into the street, along the road, toward the main road. With Freddy walking alongside and guiding it, and Benson behind, they pushed until they were some distance away from the Morencys' house. Then Tisdale got in. A moment later, he exclaimed:

"Our night out, Syd—he's left the keys in!"

Benson actually chuckled.

They started off.

Three hundred yards farther on, they came to a main road. They needed to turn left, for London. As they nosed out of the side turning, they looked both ways. No more than half a mile along toward Stoke, on a straight stretch of road, were several red lights, some yellow lights, and the shadowy shapes of men and cars.

"Road block," breathed Freddy Tisdale. "If we'd gone the other way . . ."

"Well, we didn't" Benson said flatly. "We'll drive on the sidelights only; if there's another block down the road they won't see us coming so far, and we'll have a chance to stop and run for it."

Freddy didn't speak.

With the sidelights on, casting only a faint glow on the hedges, the telegraph poles and the wires, they crawled along at twenty miles an hour. Occasionally, a car passed them; once, one came streaking up from behind, and whined past; it didn't stop.

Freddy knew the roads well, took the byroads, avoided the towns where the police road blocks were likely to be, and by half past five they reached the outskirts of Birmingham.

In Birmingham, Freddy had a hide-out, with a man he felt sure was safe. Or so he said.

Gideon entered the office, next morning, a little more briskly than usual. There was no reason why he should feel in high spirits, but he did. Possibly the overnight news of the capture of two more prisoners had something to do with it. Possibly, eight hours' solid sleep had helped; possibly, too, amused reflection on Pru's high color when she had come in and again when he had seen her at breakfast that morning. She had asked about William Rose, but had her own absorbing personal interests now. Gideon wondered how long she had known this Raymond, told himself that he would have to make sure that the youngster was all right, then thought reassuringly that Kate would make certain of that, as far as anyone could.

He saw Lemaitre, alone at his desk, with the daily report in front of him.

"Morning, Lem."

"Morning, George." Lemaitre was flat-voiced, gloomy.

"What's your trouble?"

"Trouble?" asked Lemaitre, and gave a laugh which had no body in it. "Nothing but ruddy trouble, if you ask me. Had a hell of a row with Fifi last night; she wanted to go out, and I wanted to stay in—George, you don't know how lucky you are."

Lemaitre had graver marital troubles even than he realized; but Gideon didn't see that it was his duty to tell him.

"She'll be all right tonight," he said, soothingly.

"Sometimes I wonder," said Lemaitre, "sometimes I wonder if—oh, forget it. We picked up Alderman and Hooky last night, that's something. Manchester police say there's blood on Alderman's clothes and under his fingernails, mixed with coal dust. We've got them ready for the long wait." That prospect seemed to cheer Lemaitre up. "Twenty-nine spots of bother in London last night, and we've picked up five old pals who'll be in dock this morning. Young Rose will be up at East London, of course— medical reports on him in from Smedd, in triplicate— Smedd's a boy! Nasty job in Soho: one of the Marlborough Street regulars cut up. The risks these women take at that game. Nasty job out at Wimbledon, too: nineteen-year-old girl going home after a dance; had a tiff with her boy friend and she went alone. Three fellows had a go at her. Sometimes I wonder what makes men tick, I do really. She got home all right, not hurt except for a few bruises and scratches; she put up a hell of a fight. Kept her head better than a lot would, too: described one of the fellows and said he had a foreign accent. The Wimbledon police boys are checking, they think they can put their hands on the trio. Nice morning, isn't it?"

"If you didn't want to know all about the seamy side, why join the police?" asked Gideon.

He looked through the newspapers. As he'd expected, the "negligence" at Millways was being tied up to the "negligence" at Brixton; the escapes and the prison suicide were being run together as clear indications of lowered standards at the prisons. There was a sly dig at the police for allowing a party of violent criminals to remain at large, but the capture of Alderman and Hooky won a corner in the Stop Press.

Then Gideon read his own daily report.

He made notes and, before he started the morning's briefing, studied the medical reports on William Rose. One was from his family doctor, and it was a long statement; the doctor had known the Rose family for twenty-five years.

Should be reliable.

Gideon read—and winced.

Penciled in red at the side of the report were the letters N.B. Opposite this, there was the blunt statement:

From the age of six until the age of eleven the boy showed signs of excessive, uncontrollable temper. His mother brought him to me for treatment, but this was clearly not a matter for an ordinary physician. I understand that the boy responded well to psychiatric treatment, becoming much more balanced. I questioned his mother on a number of occasions in later years, and was told that there were no further outbreaks of this particular trouble.

Well, well; a history of violent temper. Dig deeper, and this would probably show that Rose flew into rages, possibly that he had been uncontrollable; a mother wouldn't be likely to take a six-year-old boy to a doctor unless it was for some quite exceptional tantrums. No wonder Smedd had written N.B. The family doctor's purpose stood out a mile, of course; he was establishing a history of mental unbalance because he was afraid that young Rose had killed the girl, and that the state of his mind would be of vital importance at the trial.

Not good for Pru's "friend," or for William Rose.

And obviously Smedd had no fresh news about the couple visiting the cinema, or about the "lost" knife.

In the middle of the morning Gideon sent for Lefty Bligh, who had been up at Great Marlborough Street, and remanded for the constitutional eight days. Now that he was over his shock, he was smiling.

"Hallo, Guv-ner, now don't you start," he greeted.

"You're a mutton-headed fool, Lefty," Gideon said, "but I don't suppose anything will cure you now. Heard from Syd Benson lately?"

Lefty's whole expression changed.

"Mr. Gideon," he said earnestly, "I wouldn't have no more truck with that man for a fortune."

"How about making us out a list of his friends? It might help you next week if you did."

The little thief's eyes were filled with reproach which would have made any other man than a policeman believe he was of great virtue.

"Now would I squeal, Mr. Gideon? Even if I knew any of Benson's pals, you know I wouldn't."

It had been worth trying; but as an informer, Lefty was a dead loss. So, to Gideon, was the rest of that afternoon. He just couldn't get the line he wanted so desperately; and each hour that Benson remained free increased his wife's danger.

Young Syd Benson saw Abbott outside the house in Muskett Street that afternoon, glared at him, and then walked along the street toward the corner and toward his school for the afternoon lessons. Abbott followed. It was his first experience of watching a youngster, and he was beginning to realize how difficult a strong-willed boy could make the job. Coming from school that morning, Syd had dawdled along, had jeered and derided Abbott in mime, had talked about flaming coppers, narks and flat-foots to his friends, and generally shown off. Annoyed at first, Abbott had gradually become philosophical, accepting this as inevitable.

He'd already told Gideon that he wasn't happy about the boy, and at that time Gideon was Abbott's Hero number one.

Halfway along Muskett Street on his way back to school, young Syd tried a new dodge: he broke into a run.

Abbott saw that, and hesitated for a split second. The

boy was off to a flying start, and could run like a hare. Abbott, who hadn't sprinted for years but who still played a useful game of football, lost time in trying to decide whether he should lose what was left of his dignity by running, or whether he should let the little brute get away.

He ran.

There were a dozen or so other children in the street, all heading toward school, several mothers, two men on bicycles, and a milkman's van. Everyone stopped to stare at the pounding policeman and the running boy. Young Syd reached the corner at least fifty yards ahead, and took time off to turn round and put his thumb to his nose. That started a roar of laughter followed by jeers and catcalls.

"Hit one your own size, can't you?"

"Catch him, cowboy!"

"How're your flat feet, copper?"

Abbott set his teeth and ran on, going very fast now, much faster than the boy could. Provided he was still in the street which bisected this one, Syd wouldn't get away. Abbott neared the corner, and then saw one of the cyclists draw up alongside him. The cyclist was grinning, but he didn't speak. He passed Abbott and, a yard or so in front of him, his bicycle wobbled. He made it do that deliberately, but no one would ever be able to prove it. As if trying to keep his balance, he crossed Abbott's path; the detective looked as if he would crash into him.

Abbott saw the danger in time.

He pulled himself up, inches from the bicycle, and managed to spin round on one foot, as he would on the football field if the ball ran the wrong way. To save himself from falling, he thrust out his right hand, and caught the cyclist on the shoulder. He felt the man give way, heard him bellow, saw him leap for the pavement. Something clutched at Abbott's coat, but did no harm. He didn't look round, but heard the cyclist crash, and then realized that the catcalls had stopped.

He reached the corner.

Young Syd was playing marbles with two other boys; he grinned impudently.

Abbott, gasping for breath, could have wrung the boy's neck. He stopped, standing by the wall of a house, hearing a gabble of voices round the corner. From a distance, a uniformed policeman from the Division came hurrying, and if there was anything that a Divisional man enjoyed it was a Yard man being made to look silly.

The crowd in Muskett Street would be after him for this, too. The cyclist would almost certainly try to make trouble. Abbott, trying to put the detective before the human being, saw through all this to his chief job: keeping an eye on the boy. He would have to leave the constable to make a kind of peace with the crowd, but was afraid that from now on he would be jeered at by everyone in Muskett Street.

The cyclist turned the corner, back on his machine. His right hand was bleeding from a nasty scratch. He glowered at Abbott, and said roughly, "Why the hell don't you look where you're going?"

Abbott gaped—and then found the wit to say: "Sorry. Didn't see you."

A woman, just out of sight, laughed—at the cyclist, not Abbott. The man pedaled off; and as he watched him go, Abbott realized what had happened. Just when he'd feared the worst, he'd had a break. If he'd fallen and the cyclist ridden on triumphantly, he would have been the fool; but in Muskett Street as well as in the whole of London there was admiration for the man who got out of a tight corner; and there was an innate sense of fair play.

Abbott felt on top of the world.

A woman turned the corner, then. She was middle-aged, dressed in a bright blue dress of some shiny material, and she wore a black straw hat trimmed with bright red cherries. She had a huge, tightly confined bosom and a surprisingly small waist; a red, beery face and little brown eyes. She swept round the corner, spotted Abbott and then young Syd, and strode toward Benson's son, ignoring the marbles. She caught one with the toe of her shoe, and it went skimming to the other side of the street.

"Now you listen to me, young Sydney," she said in a voice loud enough to be heard up and down the street. "If you was my boy I'd give you a clip round the ear and keep on doing it until I knocked some sense into you. The gentleman's only trying to help you, see? Help you and your Ma and Liz, which is a damned sight more than your father's ever done. If he'd earned an honest living, instead of taking up with a lot of loose women and neglecting your Ma and then going off to prison and leaving her to look after the pair of you, there'd have been some sense. But he never did have any sense, and by the looks of it you haven't got much, neither. Don't you forget it, this gentleman's only doing his duty, and trying to help you."

She stopped, on a high-pitched note.

Syd's bright blue eyes were not turned toward her, but toward Abbott.

"I don't want his flipping help," he said, and swung away.

Young Syd, fuming at the way the woman had talked to him, fuming at the way his mother had rebuked him, hating Abbott, resenting everything that had happened to his father, walked on toward school that afternoon. He was alone except for one boy, a big, gangling lad named Simon who, many people thought, should not be allowed near the school. But he was harmless enough, and had short-lived periods of intelligence. Most of his time he spent in a special school, but at playtime he was allowed in here, with the others.

Abbott, following, would not have been surprised had young Syd played truant; but he went on to school. There were only two exits, and the police watched each; it was likely to be a boring afternoon for Abbott.

It wasn't boring for young Syd.

In the playground thronged with a mob of shouting, running boys, he stood watching, brooding, with Simon near him, gawping about with his mouth hanging open. It was one of his bad days.

Another boy came up.

No one but the gangling lad was near, and he was out of earshot.

The second boy said, "Got a message for you, Syd," in a voice which showed that he was swelling with importance.

"You can keep it," said Syd sourly.

"You'll wish you hadn't said that."

"Listen, Charlie, I don't want to talk to you or no one, get to hell out of here, can't you?"

"Okay, okay," said Charlie, and backed away a yard; young Syd could box! "It's a message from my Dad, though, he says it's important. He'd have given it to you himself, only he knows the cops are watching you."

Young Syd's eyes lost their viciousness in a momentary flicker of interest.

"What's it all about?"

"Dad wants to see you tonight, without the cops knowing, see. Can you make it?"

"The flippin' busies watch me all the time."

"That's what Dad said," went on young Charlie, "but it's okay. You've got to climb over the school wall into the builder's yard. Someone'll be waiting in a van, you nip inside the van and you'll be okay. Dad says it's important."

Syd's eyes were shining.

"Okay," he said, "okay."

Abbott didn't see the boy, after school. The rest of the children came out, but not Syd Benson. The teachers came out, too. It wasn't until Benson had been missing for over half an hour that another boy was found who had seen him climb into the builder's yard next to the school.

There was no trace of him now.

13 . Clues

Gideon heard Abbott's voice, low-pitched and completely lacking the bright eagerness which had been there before. From a long-term point of view, this wouldn't do Abbott any harm; it was never a bad thing to have a job go sour on you in the early days, and too long a run of early successes could do a lot of harm. But it was a thousand pities he had to learn his lesson on this job.

Obviously, Abbott had done everything that could be done at short notice.

"All right, and don't forget it isn't the end of the world," Gideon said. "I'll have a word with the Division. We've got a woman watching young Liz, so you switch over to Mrs. Benson and that man of hers, Arthur Small. Know him?"

"Yes, sir, if you remember, I reported last night . . ."

"Oh, yes," said Gideon. "All right. Good-by."

He rang off, and found himself looking down at a photograph, which had come in only a little while ago, of Arthur Small, who was in charge of the shop where Ruby Benson worked. The shop was one of a chain, with a male manager and female staff; there were three assistants junior to Ruby, as well as Small. Small was in the late forties, rather dapper, and in his way good-looking. He was going a little thin on top, and wore horn-rimmed glasses which gave his face a top-heavy look. Gideon, knowing that it was more than just an affair between him and Ruby, wondered how it would end. Even when Benson was caught, Ruby would be tied to him; she and Small couldn't get married.

The reports on Small were all excellent.

He had been questioned, and had said flatly that he was going to stay at Ruby's house from now until Benson was caught, and if the police didn't like it, they could lump it. That showed spirit if nothing else.

But young Syd . . .

Gideon put everything in hand: a widespread search, photographs of the boy to the newspapers, questioning of the schoolmasters and the other boys; but no reports came in. The builder's men were questioned, but no one admitted having seen young Syd. It was a complete blank, and Gideon didn't like it.

Benson might be in London; might have got hold of the boy; might be within a mile or so of the Yard.

Benson wasn't; that night, the third of freedom, he spent lying low in a house on the outskirts of Birmingham, with Freddy Tisdale. It was quite a night, for they had feminine company.

The body still lay under the little car on the cold ground and so far the snow had prevented any serious degree of decomposition.

No one else visited the furnished house.

Reports of the theft of a car from the car park near Millways, and of the theft of a car from a private garage on the outskirts of Stoke, reached the Yard in the usual way. Obviously, it was possible that one of the escaped men had taken these, but a dozen cars or more had been stolen from the same area during the past week.

Both cars were found within twenty-four hours. There were no fingerprints in either of them; but in the one found in the Stoke car park there was a little roll of parking tickets of the kind used to refill the machines used at Millways Corporation. The fact that the car park attendant was missing had also been reported; the general belief was that he had absconded. During the first and second days of his disappearance, those councillors and Council officials who had opposed the employment of an ex-convict were loud in their righteousness and in the vigor of their "We told you so."

Then, on the fourth morning, a dog, howling and sniffing, led an elderly man to the car park attendant's body.

"My God," breathed Gideon.

Now they had something to get their teeth into. The stolen car was quickly connected with the old lag's murder; it was clear that a pair of the prisoners had got as far south as Stoke, probable that they had gone farther south. Then a man from the Stoke Police Department's Fingerprints Bureau, checking the second stolen car, found not fingerprints but glove prints.

"Pigskin or imitation pigskin, with a cut in the thumb and worn on the inside edge of the thumb," he said in his report, which reached Gideon on the afternoon of the fourth day.

Soon reports began to flow in.

The police knew what they were looking for, had confirmation from Alderman and Hooky that the other four had gone off in pairs, knew that one of the two wore pigskin gloves, and realized that meant that they had probably got hold of other clothes. A Millways C.I.D. man, trying to find out if clothes had been taken from the scene of any local burglary, learned instead that some food had been stolen from a grocery shop near the canal. The shopkeeper and his wife were quite sure, because they had been taking stock on the night before they'd made the discovery, and had counted the half-pound packets of butter and some packets of bicuits. They had suspected a sneak thief, and hadn't reported the missing food until they'd heard that the police were anxious to know about every kind of theft on the night of the big prison break.

Two glove thumbprints, identical with those discovered on the stolen cars, were found on tins of soup and beneath a shelf in the shop. Immediately, this news brought a concentration of police to the canal area. A sergeant who took the routine in his stride collected all the keys of nearby furnished houses from the agents.

Benson's first hiding-place was found, and the report sped to London.

"Now we're really moving," Gideon said, and he felt a fierce excitement. "Benson's prints were all over the house, so were Tisdale's. We've a list of the clothes that have been stolen, size of shoes, hats, everything. There was a careful inventory made before the owners left the place empty; we've got the description down to the last detail."

"Spread 'em around," said Lemaitre, and rubbed his hands together. "We'll soon pick the swine up now."

They were not picked up that night, for they were in Birmingham; reveling.

Young Syd wasn't found, either.

The Assistant Commissioner, often a late bird, looked into Gideon's office about half past nine that night, and found Gideon there alone. That wasn't unusual. Gideon had a mass of reports in front of him, and looked up from the one he was reading: a psychiatrist's report on William Rose, the same psychiatrist who had attended him in his childhood. Gideon put it aside, stretched back in his chair, and then bent down and opened a cupboard.

"I know what you're after," he said. "One of these days I'm going to put a fresh item on the expense sheet—one bottle of whisky for official consumption!" He put a bottle on the desk, then a siphon, then two glasses. "If you want to know what I think," he went on, "I think this is one of the lousiest weeks I've ever had at the Yard."

The A.C. looked at the gurgling whisky.

"They all seem like that," he said. "Don't let it get you down, George."

Gideon pushed a glass toward him.

"Oh, it'll pass, but it's like seeing a blank wall every way you look. I did think we'd get something when we found out where Benson had been and what clothes he was wearing, but—well, mustn't expect miracles, I suppose."

"What's really upset you?" the A.C. asked. "Not the newspaper?"

"If I had my way, I'd dump all crime reporters in the sea," growled Gideon, and then unexpectedly he laughed. "Oh, we can't blame 'em! Four violent criminals still free, then Edmundsun, and then young Benson. No wonder we're making headlines. Chap I'm sorry for is Abbott," he went on. "Seems to think it's nobody's fault but his."

"Like Gideon, like Abbott," the A.C. said, and gave his quick grin. "Funny thing about that boy, though. No sign of him?"

"No. I'm as worried as hell."

"Think someone's hiding him?"

"He could have found a spot to keep under cover by himself, I suppose," said Gideon thoughtfully, "but as far as his mother knows, he had only about sixpence on him, and kids get hungry. If I had to bet, it'd be that he went to a place where he knew he'd be looked after. We've checked all of Benson's friends, and haven't got anywhere at all. He nipped over into that builder's yard, and just hasn't been seen since. The yard opens onto the Mile End Road, dozens of people pass it every hour of the day, and we haven't picked up one who saw the kid."

"Think Benson's had anything to do with it?"

"I think Benson's had something to do with everything," said Gideon, savoring his whisky. "But then, I've a Benson obsession at the moment. That man's running round with a knife, and there isn't a better knife artist in the country—the way he killed that poor devil near Millways shows that. One thrust, and it went right home. He wouldn't need long to kill his wife or her beau."

The A.C. said, "That's not like you, George. You know he'll never get near enough."

Gideon shrugged. "Unless he's soon caught, I'll believe that anything's possible. But you're right, of course; it's not reasonable."

"No. What about this Primrose Girl murder?"

Gideon tapped the report he had been reading. "I've never read a case which looked more open and shut," he said. "There's a clear medical history of mental instability when a child, there's all the evidence that Smedd's accumulated, and except for one thing, it looks foolproof."

"What's the one thing?"

"Rose's sister's story. Nothing shakes it. And Rose himself sticks to it, too—as well as his lost knife story. He says he had this quarrel with Winnie Norton in the woods, left her in a temper, went toward his home, feeling like hell, and met his sister; and she treated him to the pictures. There's no doubt at all that if they went into those pictures Rose didn't kill the girl. Death was at about seven o'clock—the broken watch as well as medical evidence proves that. Mary Rose says she and her brother were inside the picture palace before six—and it's pretty certain that the girl really was there. It was a busy evening, there were dozens going in just about that time, and a hundred or so coming out. The girl can describe every film, the shorts, the news, the cartoon and the advertisements—she even remembers one of the tunes on the record player during the interval! If her brother was with her, he couldn't have killed that girl. Smedd says that he's done everything possible to find anyone who saw either the girl or her brother, without result. And that's the element of doubt," Gideon went on. "If someone had seen her without her brother, we'd know where we are. But she was there. She'd announced she was going beforehand, and it's as near a certainty as a thing can be. If she wasn't noticed, then the pair of them might not have been."

"See what you mean," said the A.C. "That's all that's on your mind?"

"I've got a lot of stuff going through the courts tomorrow," Gideon told him. "Nine C.I.s, as many D.I.s and twelve sergeants are all scheduled to give evidence in one court or other. Falling over each other. Old Birdy will be back in Number One, and Lemaitre will have to go there. We had a squeak that there'll be a bullion raid at the London Airport tomorrow, so I've sent half a dozen men up to watch. It's probably a false alarm, but we can't take risks. Take it from me, we could have handled the Benson job much better last week; just now we're stretched as far as we can go. And if there wasn't enough on our plate, there's that attempted rape job out at Wimbledon."

"Unrelieved gloom," the Assistant Commissioner observed; but his looks belied him. "What have you been working late on?"

"Had a session with young Cummings," said Gideon. "He says he's got a feeling that the Edmundsun job will spread a long way before it's over. I'm seeing Edmundsun's wife tomorrow. Cummings thinks she might know who her husband was working with . . ."

The A.C. stopped him with a laugh.

"George," he said, "I'm not going to let you get away with that one. I was talking to Lemaitre, and he told me you put Cummings up to it. Think it'll work?"

"From what I can gather, the wife was in love with him," said Gideon, smiling. "Bit of a spitfire, and if she thinks she's got anyone to hate, she'll hate."

"I'll leave it to you," the A.C. conceded. "Now if I were you, I'd go home; it's late."

"Can't grumble about this week," Gideon said. "I've been home for supper two nights out of three, and I'll be home in time for a nightcap tonight." He stood up, and stifled a yawn. "Any truth in the rumor that you're likely to retire?" He smiled as he looked straight into the A.C.'s face. "I've been reading the Sunday Sentinel, you see."

"That's one of the things I came to have a word with

you about," the A.C. said quietly. "No, George, I'm not retiring yet. I always planned to have seven years, if they didn't throw me out, and I've four to go. That should make you about fifty-three when you take over, and you ought to hold the job down for eleven or twelve years."

"They won't put me in your place," Gideon said flatly.

"They'll be bloody fools if they don't," said the other man and finished his whisky. "Good night!"

Gideon went through the brightly-lit corridors of the quiet building. Down below, in the Information Room, they would be busier now than at any time during the day; the night's crop of crimes was being reported. In Fingerprints and Records, in the Photographic Division, in Ballistics—in fact everywhere on the C.I.D. section, there would be experts at work, more than at some periods during the day; and yet you couldn't make night into day, the place had a dead look. The clerical staff weren't here, of course, and the administrative staff were out at the pictures or watching television or listening to the radio, at church socials, at their hobbies, or perhaps cuddling. Gideon grinned at himself, and had a sneaking thought that he was getting a bit too prosy.

He drove home at a steady pace.

Kate, Prudence, Priscilla and Matthew were still up, having a hand of whist. Tom, the oldest son, was working in the north of England, and only came home occasionally; Malcolm, the nine-year-old, was in bed. Gideon watched the game, winked at Kate when he saw her play the wrong card and so give Priscilla a trick, and then sat back in his armchair. Pleasant. There were times when this seemed to be the only part of life that wasn't seamy.

Yet William Rose had spread his influence here.

What was the truth about that boy?

It was a little before midnight when Gideon went to bed, and Kate looked through the newspapers as he undressed. She didn't pester him, but he could see that she read the reports about young Syd Benson closely. He told her that there was no trace of the boy.

By half past twelve they were both asleep.

At two o'clock the telephone bell rang.

Gideon was in the deep sleep of the early hours, and heard the sound as through a thick mist. Then he felt something stir. Next he felt Kate leaning across him, her breast against his shoulder. He fought to open his eyes, and grunted to let her know that he was waking up. She said something, then switched on the light near the telephone.

"It's something about those prisoners."

In that instant, Gideon was wide awake.

"They got the others?" He snatched the telephone. "Hallo, Gideon speaking . . ."

"Where?" he breathed.

Kate saw his expression, the tightening of his lips, the way the muscles at the side of his face worked. His eyes no longer looked sleepy. He said, "Okay, I'll come right away," and put the receiver down. Kate didn't say: "George, must you?" but started to get out of bed.

"You needn't get up," Gideon protested.

"I'm going to make you a cup of tea, you're not going out at this hour without something to warm you."

He grunted, "Thanks."

"It isn't Benson, is it?"

"No, two of the others—Jingo Smith and Matt Owens," Gideon told her. "They've been traced to a warehouse and factory near the docks, locked themselves in the laboratory, and threaten to blow the place up if the police don't let 'em go. Blurry fools," growled Gideon, "but it's the kind of thing Jingo Smith would try, he always was a flamboyant fool. The lunatics didn't send for me until the last minute, they've the fire brigade out and half the police force, I shouldn't wonder."

Kate said, "Oh."

"You don't have to worry," said Gideon, and stared at her in surprise, for she looked almost frightened. "Here, Kate, I'll be all right."

From the door she said, "Sometimes I wonder if you know what fear is. Get your clothes on, and don't forget that woolly waistcoat, it's cold tonight."

"Well," grinned Gideon, "you should know, you're wearing nylon and not much else." He tossed her his own woolen dressing gown, and then turned round to dress.

14 . Cornered

The streets near the warehouse had been cordoned off, and it wasn't until he had been recognized that Gideon was allowed to go through. As he drew nearer the warehouse, he saw the fire engines with their ladders up and two men perched on a turntable that seemed to be a vast distance up in the starlit sky. The shapes of tall ware-houses, of cranes and of the masts of ships showed up dark against the stars. There were the sounds inseparable from a massed crowd of people. Uniformed police and several plain-clothes men stood around, and one after another they saluted Gideon. He drove slowly to a point where there was no room to pass other cars, got out, and walked toward a little group of men near the surrounded ware-house. Car headlights and one ship's searchlight shone on the walls and the windows of this place, and the light was reflected from the glass. Not far from the spot where the group of men waited was an ambulance; two men were being given first aid.

Gideon drew up.

"Anyone hurt badly?" he asked sharply.

Trabert, the Yard man who had summoned him, and the Divisional C.I., named Wilson, turned round at the sound of his voice.

"Hallo, George," the Yard man greeted. "Sorry we didn't call you earlier, didn't think they'd be such fools. It depends what you call badly—one chap's got a knife wound in his shoulder and another a cracked skull. Nice lot, those Millways chaps."

"Seen 'em?"

"No. They're in that corner over there." Trabert, a thinnish, graying man whose overcoat looked too large for him, pointed to a corner. "There's a laboratory up there, with steel doors, and they've closed the doors. Only way we can get at them is through the window. They've got enough nitroglycerin to blow the place sky-high, and they could start a fire that would burn out half London. Been talking to the chief chemist, and he says the stuff's there all right." Trabert had always a reputation for being pic-turesque, and for exaggeration. "I've talked to the pair on the radio with a loud-speaker, and they've got a mega-phone up there."

Gideon looked at the window.

"Any of our chaps inside?"

"I ordered them out. If the place does go up, I'd rather we didn't have a lot of casualties."

"Wouldn't be a bad idea if you moved back a bit your-self," said Gideon. He looked at the dim light, and he tried to picture the two men inside. Jingo Smith was as hard as they were made; a good second to Benson. The man with him, Matt Owens, had no record of violence;

but probably he knew that if he were caught his sentence would be so long that it was worth making desperate efforts to stay free.

At heart, each man must know that he hadn't really a chance.

But they could do a lot of damage before giving in.

"Don't mind admitting it was my own fault," said Wilson. The Divisional man had a gruff, whispering voice. "I had a flash from one of our chaps, saying they were here, and thought I'd be clever. Didn't realize that Smith and Owens knew they'd been seen, so I thought I'd pull them in, and make you a present. I ought to be hamstrung."

Gideon said, "Who doesn't make a boner, some time or other?" It was the only thing he could say, although inwardly he felt the welling up of bitterness against a responsible officer who had taken risks simply to cover himself, or his Division, with glory. Some men didn't seem to grow up. "Well, we'd better call the A.C. and let him have a word with a big shot at the Home Office."

Wilson said, "Listen, George, let me go and have a try to reason with them."

"In a minute," Gideon said. "Anyone here from the warehouse, to tell us how to get inside from the roof or the back?"

"George," said Trabert, quietly, "there's only one way in now—through that window. We can't break down a steel door, armor plating couldn't be tougher. If you and anyone else try heroics, you'll be crazy. We could try to hose them out, but if we do they might toss some nitroglycerin down. If it comes to that, we might knock a tube of the damned stuff off a bench, and start the blow-up that way. There isn't any way of getting into that laboratory. We'll have to starve them out."

He stopped.

Then a loud voice sounded from the direction of the window. Gideon and every other man stared toward it and the ladder which leaned against the wall near it. No one appeared; but Gideon saw the round mouth of a megaphone, like those used on the docks when foremen dockers needed to make themselves heard above a din.

"Hi there, Gee-Gee!" That was Jingo Smith. "Didn't think it would be long before they got you out of bed. How do you like it?"

Gideon—George Gideon made Gee-Gee inevitable, and he was often surprised that it wasn't used more—put his great hands to his mouth and called back in a voice which was almost as powerful as Jingo Smith's when amplified by the megaphone. At least fifty people were standing, watching and listening; and more were arriving every minute.

"I don't like it at all, Jingo," Gideon called. "I never like to see a man make a fool of himself."

"I'm no fool," Jingo called back. His weakness, the weakness of so many of them, was vanity. Now he was the center of attraction, and having a wonderful time. It was at least possible that he had managed to get drunk, if only on methylated spirits from the laboratory. There would probably be pure alcohol there, too, and he wouldn't lose any time finding out. "They told you what I'm going to do?"

"No, what's it to be?"

"They *didn't* tell you? What's the matter, they gone deaf? This is what it will be, Gee-Gee! I've got a tube of nitro in my pocket, and I'm going to bring it out with me. Anyone who tries to stop me will get it—and that goes for anyone within a fifty-foot radius, too. Any copper want to come to hell with me? Why don't you come, Gee-Gee?"

"Give it a rest," Gideon called. "You can't get away, and you know it. Better have a few more years up at Millways than blow yourself to pieces."

"Gee-Gee," bawled Jingo Smith, "we're coming out in ten minutes; and if anyone gets near us, up will go the balloon."

Gideon didn't speak for at least a minute; everyone within earshot was waiting for him; the tension in the street was like an electric current. Then, just as Smith was going to speak again—they actually heard him clear his throat—Gideon tossed back his great head and bellowed:

"Owens, do you want to be blown to Kingdom Come? Hit him over the head, and knock some sense into him! You'll get off lightly if you do."

Silence.

Would Matt Owens have the nerve . . .

Then: "No, you don't!" screamed Jingo Smith. "I'll smash your face . . ."

His voice fell to a whisper as he dropped the megaphone. Gideon didn't need to speak, but led the rush toward the ladder—Trabert, Wilson and two other men following at speed. They heard the scuffling inside. Behind them there was an awful silence; one which might be broken by a blast which could kill the men in the room and the policemen who were so near. Gideon reached the ladder and climbed up it as fast as any fireman. He heard the gasping and the scuffling. He reached the top of the ladder and could see inside the laboratory as he flashed his flashlight beam into the room.

Jingo Smith and Matt Owens were on the floor, rolling over and over. The megaphone lay near them. The light of the torch flashed on the glass of beakers, burettes, glass tubes, bottles, on Bunsen burners, on all the paraphernalia of the laboratory. A dim electric light burned in a corner, near the men.

Gideon thrust the window up.

He heard bottles rattling. He saw a dozen tubes on one of the benches, shaking when the fighting men rolled against it. He didn't know, and couldn't tell for certain, whether there was nitroglycerin in one of those tubes; he only knew that if there was, and it fell, he wouldn't have anything more to worry about.

He slid into the room.

Jingo Smith brought a bottle down on Owens' head, and as Owens went still, jumped toward the bench with his hand outstretched. There was no doubt that he wanted the small, metal tube which stood there, rocking gently, halfway between the convict and Gideon.

15 . Hero

Gideon knew exactly what he had to do, exactly what the risk was. It was easy, now, to be heroic, for he had no choice. He had to bring Jingo Smith down, and had to stop him from jolting the laboratory bench. The tube was within a yard of Smith's outstretched hands; and he was looking toward it, lips distended, eyes shimmering. Matt Owens lay on the floor, writhing, yet staring at the tube with the fear of death in his eyes.

Gideon thrust out his right leg, huge foot plumb on Smith's stomach, and shoved with all his massive strength. Smith gave a thin squeal of sound and, his fingers only inches from the tube, staggered away from it. He looked like a man who was staggering away from salvation.

He wasn't finished.

He grabbed at a beaker on the bench, trying to slide it along the bench toward the tube. Gideon saw it, grabbed, and snatched up the beaker. Smith, still staggering, went closer to Owens. Owens shot out a hand and grabbed his ankle; and Smith pitched forward, arms waving wildly, and the tube still within his reach.

Gideon got between him and the bench. Smith fell heavily. Gideon, breathing very hard, went down, heaved the man over onto his stomach, and then chopped with the side of the hand at the nape of his neck. Smith lost consciousness as swiftly as a doused light goes out. The only sound was Owen's gasping breath, Gideon's hissing, and a clattering noise as someone else climbed in at the window. Gideon looked round to see Wilson, who was also gasping, and Trabert on the ladder just behind him.

Gideon looked at the tube of nitroglycerin.

"What did we bring the fire unit for?" he asked. "We can do it just as well ourselves. Don't start rocking the boat, or we'll all go under." He picked up the tube, looked round, and saw a small safe with a steel door standing open. Inside it were other tubes like this, as well as containers which held many things he didn't recognize. Without appearing to take exceptional care, he carried the tube to the safe and saw that inside, on the bottom, there were a number of holes into which tubes like this could be placed so that there was no risk of knocking them down. "Funny thing," he said heavily, "people live every day doing a job which would blow them to Kingdom Come if anything went wrong."

Other police were climbing in.

Matt Owens was getting to his feet, and a hefty D.I. grabbed his arm.

"Take it easy with Matt," Gideon said; "if it hadn't been for him we'd all be bits and pieces. Matt, if you go on being sensible, we'll get you off serious punishment for the break. If you take my advice you'll see your sentence out quietly and give yourself a chance of getting along afterward; we'll help you all we can after this. Had any food lately?"

Owens looked desperately tired.

"Hardly a bite since we got away," he said hoarsely; "squeezed into a freight train, been halfway round the ruddy country." He was shivering, only partly with cold, for he wore an old, tattered coat and beneath it what looked like a new pair of flannel trousers. "Jingo was drunk, Mr. Gideon; he put down half a pint of meth and then he found some alcohol in that bottle. He wouldn't have been so crazy if he hadn't been drunk."

"It's a good thing you kept sober," Gideon said with feeling. "We'll get you a square meal before we send you home. Take him across to the café at the end of the road," he added to two D.I.'s. "Keep him away from the newspapermen if you can."

"They don't want Owens," Trabert said, grinning and showing very big, shiny teeth. "They want you. Didn't you know you're a hero?"

There he was, too.

Every late edition of the morning newspaper, carried a photograph of Gideon, C.I.D. There were flamboyant accounts of what he had done during the night, as well as what he had done in the past. The headlines about Edmundsun and the prison escapes miraculously vanished. The Daily Globe spread itself with a leader on the daily dangers which faced the police, and cited the Gideon capture of Jingo Smith, the policeman who had stopped the New Bond Street raiders, and the Putney policeman who had rescued the woman and her child. It was enough to make Gideon purr; enough to make everyone at the Yard go about grinning, as if a big load had been lifted from everyone's mind. To help, the weather turned not only warm but fine. May had come some weeks ahead of itself.

That day, the fifth since the escape of the men from Millways, was one of the best Gideon had known for a long time. Small things went right. There were seven cases up for trial at the Old Bailey, with three of them doubtful in the outcome; the police knew they had the right man but weren't sure they had a strong enough case. Each went smoothly, each man was found guilty. Birdy, the judge in Number One Court at the Old Bailey, must have read the newspapers; he included a few sentences of congratulation to the police at the end of the case which he'd been hearing for a week. Cummings alone was less happy: he felt more sure than ever that Elliott, Edmundsun's manager, had also been Edmundsun's accomplice, but seemed less confident that he would ever be able to prove it.

About noon, on that fifth day, he came in to see Gideon.

"Don't really know that I ought to say this to you, sir," he said, "but I get a nasty feeling about the whole job. A smell, if you know what I mean. As if Elliott's covered up a cesspit and I can't make him take the cover off. When are you seeing Mrs. Edmundsun, sir?"

"Why?"

"I don't know that I should leave it too long, they might get at her."

Gideon said very slowly: "You serious?"

"All I know, sir," said Cummings, looking more flabby and pale and ill-at-ease than usual, "is that I'm not happy about it. I know it's a bit tough trying to make her talk, with her husband only just buried, but if Elliott or anyone else is going to get at her, they won't let sentiment stand in the way."

"I'll go and see her now," Gideon promised.

That was easy. The Edmundsuns had lived in a block of flats in Bayswater, comfortable but not luxurious. Gideon went right away, on his own. A maid opened the door and let him in; he waited in a room which overlooked a garden, vivid green grass and wintry-looking trees, until Mrs. Edmundsun came in. He had only seen her from her photographs, and wasn't really surprised that she looked not only different but much more attractive. She wasn't exactly a beauty, but had a figure that didn't come very often, and she had beautiful gray eyes.

"I'd hoped that the police wouldn't find it necessary to worry me again, Mr. Gideon," she said, turning his card over in her fingers; and she left it at that, as if defying him to be brute enough to question a poor, defenseless woman.

"We want to help," Gideon said easily, "and one of the ways would be to clear your husband's name, Mrs. Edmundsun. All through the investigation, he declared that he was innocent—"

"And I'm sure he was."

"Well, there's one way to establish it," said Gideon, "and that's by finding the people who are responsible. For the money is missing, you know, it was paid out on dummy hire-purchase agreements. Did he ever—"

"I've told the police everything I can," said Mrs. Edmundsun, firmly. "And if you aren't satisfied, Mr. Gideon, then I really ought to consult my solicitor. As if it isn't bad enough to have lost . . ."

Her eyes began to fill with tears.

A woman in black, with a figure which the mourning dress wasn't designed to disguise, and with those beautiful eyes and that soft voice, could be as unyielding as a brick wall. Gideon sensed it, and knew at once what was worrying Cummings. This woman was supposed to have been desperately in love with her husband; all the reports which had followed the news of his death suggested that; yet here she was as cool as if the tragedy had been a year ago, not a few days.

What had caused the change?

Gideon left her, in a non-committal way, with just enough on her mind to make her wonder whether he or another police officer would soon be back. As he reached the square, and the warm sunshine fell upon him, he thought less about her than about Cummings. A man's appearance could count heavily against him, and Cummings had that paunch, that flabby double chin, the pasty face, and those rather vague-looking eyes. Yet he had "smelt" something. Gideon knew, and everyone with a flair for C.I.D. work realized it, that once in a while a man arrived with that "sense of smell"—someone who was sure a thing was wrong but couldn't get his hands on the evidence. Cummings seemed to have it; and if he did, then his appearance mustn't stand against him.

"I'll give him a few weeks on this job," Gideon said to himself; "if he can get anything out of it, he'll be set fair."

When Gideon reached the Yard, Smedd was waiting in his office, shoulders square, ginger hair bright in the sun, freckles showing up more noticeably than ever, brisk and decisive as he would always be. This was the way of it: not one but several major jobs to think about at the same time, everything to be noted and neatly pigeon-holed, ready to be brought out again when necessary.

Gideon shook hands with Smedd, and didn't show the hope that he suddenly felt. Would Smedd come in person, leaving his precious Division, unless he had news that worried him?

"Sit down, and have a cigarette," Gideon said. He wanted the man friendly, and felt better disposed toward him than he had at the beginning of the week: Smedd had finally confirmed that he was really thorough.

"Thanks," he said, and drew a little quickly, almost nervously, at his cigarette; a kind of mannerism. "I thought I'd have a word with you about this development personally, as I know of your interest."

"Good of you," murmured Gideon.

"I've got a witness who can help us about the cinema,"

Smedd said. "Young chap, about Rose's age, who went to that same performance. I've had a man at the cinema with the box-office girl, she recognized this boy as a regular twice-a-weeker."

"Yes?"

"He said he saw Mary Rose by herself," said Smedd, deliberately. "He swears black's blue that she didn't have anyone with her. Noticed her because he knows her slightly, in fact; I think he's got one of those I-love-you-from-afar crushes." That phrase sounded odd, in the brisk, clipped way in which Smedd spoke. "That's all we want to clinch things, I think. I've asked everyone about that knife, and Rose didn't say anything about it being lost. Can't trace anyone who's actually seen him with it since he's supposed to have lost it," Smedd went on candidly, "but that's not evidence."

Yes, he was thorough.

"Thing I wanted to check with you, Commander: shall I try to break the girl down now, get her to admit she was lying, or shall I wait until later? Rose is up for the second hearing on Tuesday; he'll be committed for trial, of course."

Gideon said slowly, "I think the best thing is to make sure your new witness is absolutely reliable, and then save him for the trial. We'll look for others, too—and mustn't forget that the defense is going to search high and low for someone who saw them both, or for anyone who was told that knife was lost."

Smedd shook his head swiftly, rather like a ventriloquist's puppet.

"Take it from me, the defense is going for insanity," he said. "They'll know better than to try anything else. Thing is, I'd be happier if they weren't going to put the sister up, lays a false trail—you know how it is. I'd like to let her know we know she's lying, before the trial comes up."

"Well, there's plenty of time," Gideon said. "Won't be up until June, end of May at the earliest. You certainly didn't leave much to chance."

"It isn't my habit to leave anything to chance," said Smedd, almost tartly.

Gideon didn't know that at that moment the solicitor who was looking after William Rose's interests was talking to Rose's sister and his mother, in the small suburban house on the outskirts of the H5 Division. The solicitor, an elderly man with a lifetime's experience, a rather tired manner and a shabby gray suit, was sitting in the front room, considering the mother, not Mary Rose. Mrs. Rose, at fifty-nine, looked nearer seventy: old, tired, so very, very sad.

"What Mary must understand," the solicitor said precisely, "is that the police will do everything to discredit her statement that she went with her brother to this picture house on the day and at the time in question. Now we need her as a reliable witness for the defense, we do not want her to be browbeaten by the prosecution and—ah —possibly caught out in a lie."

He shot a quick glance at Mary.

Mary said, in a quiet, stubborn voice, "They can't prove that I lied if I didn't. I met Will in the High Street, and he told me he'd had a quarrel with Winnie and hardly knew what to do with himself, he was so upset. So I treated him to the pictures, because he hadn't any money."

There was a long pause. Then:

"Mary, did you really—" began her mother.

And Gideon didn't know that, just after one o'clock that day, Arthur Small was talking to Ruby Benson in the back of the shop in the Mile End Road. Two other assistants were attending to a customer, the door was closed, and the couple kept their voices very low. They were surrounded by dresses, coats and suits, hanging inside transparent plastic cabinets all around the room. Boxes, flat now, tissue paper and balls of string were on a table in the middle of this room.

"Ruby, try not to worry so much," Small said, pleadingly. "It's making you ill, and what good will that do you or Liz? The police are bound to find young Syd sooner or later, they're bound to."

"If you knew him," Ruby said in a flat voice, "you wouldn't talk like that. He's taken the boy away from me, he's taken my own son."

Small, moving nervously about the little room, picked up a packet of cigarettes, put a cigarette to his lips, but didn't light it. It got very wet almost at once.

"Ruby, you know how I feel about you, don't you? I love you more than I love anything or anybody, but—but it isn't any use pretending about anything, is it? If young Syd can be turned against you as easily as that, then he was never very close to you, was he? He was always closer to his father." When Ruby didn't answer, Small tried to light the cigarette; it wouldn't draw. He dropped it into an ashtray, and went on, unhappily: "Ruby, I didn't mean to be unkind, but I can't bear to see you torture yourself like this. I—I'll make it up to you, you know that. If we can bring young Syd round, that'll be wonderful; but if we can't—well, we've still got Liz, and you and me together."

Ruby just looked at him.

He was older than he seemed at first sight: nearing fifty. He was rather small and white and precise, as reliable and as trustworthy as a man could be. Behind his horn-rimmed glasses, his eyes were a clear gray, steadfast, pleading. Since she had known him, he had given her not only comfort but contentment.

Now, out of her distress, she said,

"I know, Art, but—but what good am I to you? While he's alive I can't even marry you, it's not fair to you. You ought to go away and . . ."

"Don't talk like that!" Small cried; his voice was louder and sharper, and it made her stop. He took her arms, firmly. "Now listen to me, and stop this nonsense. You're getting hysterical. Supposing we can't get married? We can live together and set up house, can't we, and who's going to care whether we've got the marriage lines or not? We've both got every right to happiness, and there's no reason why we shouldn't take it. He'll be in prison for at least twelve years, after this, and I don't care what anyone says, it would be criminal for you to live on your own all that time. And—I'm—not—going—to—let—you."

His grip on her arms was very tight.

Then, suddenly, they were close to each other; she was clinging to him desperately, and crying.

Ten minutes later, she looked less haggard. Her eyes were still red from crying, but not so drawn and filled with shadows. He looked bright and perky, with a cigarette at his lips, also damp but at least giving off smoke.

"That's settled then," he said briskly; "we start the day that he's caught, and they can call it living in sin if they like. Now I must go along to see Rubenstein; if I can buy those dresses for twenty per cent less than he's asking we should make a very good profit, and that'll swell the commission." He kissed her again, and went out into the shop. The customer had gone, and the young assistants looked at him knowingly. He nodded to them, and went out. Nearby was a uniformed policeman, he was used to that.

Nearby, also, was the plain-clothes man from Scotland Yard, Abbott; Small was getting used to him. There were the usual passersby, two or three of them looking at the window of the next-door shop; and on the pavement on the Aldgate side of the shop was the simple child, Simon, badly dressed, mouth gaping, drooling a little.

No one ever took any notice of poor Simon.

"Afternoon, officer," said Arthur Small to Abbott, "no news yet?"

"Afraid there isn't, Mr. Small."

"Between you and me I'll be glad for your sake when it's over," Small said; "you must find it very boring." He had a bright look in his eyes and a perkier manner than ever, and Abbott guessed that he'd come to some kind of an agreement with Ruby Benson.

"I get paid for it," he said dryly.

They were within a few feet of Simon, when the lad took a small milk bottle with a wide mouth from his pocket. There was liquid in it that wasn't milk, but thick and oily-looking. Abbott saw that. He was near enough to strike the bottle aside, but he didn't—because it was poor Simon, and because he did not even dream that Simon might have been put up to do this.

There were some things that Simon could do well. He swung the bottle, ejecting a stream of liquid toward Arthur Small. That was the moment when Abbott realized what was happening. He cried out, and leaped forward. He felt burning spots on the back of his hand as he struck the boy's arm aside. The bottle fell; and as it fell, Small clapped his hands to his face and began to scream.

16 . Hospital Case

Gideon first heard the news when he came back from a late lunch in the pub in Cannon Row. He hadn't meant to have a heavy lunch, but Superintendent Wrexall, the senior Superintendent at the Yard, ten years older than Gideon and due to retire at the end of the year, had suggested that they should lunch together; he had a "case" he wanted to talk over. Gideon didn't know anything about this case, but couldn't very well refuse the invitation, and immediately after he had returned from the interview with Mrs. Edmundsun, he went off, leaving a list of

Do At Once items on Lemaitre's desk. A sergeant was in charge of the office until he or Lemaitre returned.

Wrexall's "case" wasn't exactly a waste of time.

While some Superintendents at the Yard specialized, like King-Hadden, of Fingerprints, most of them tackled whatever job presented itself. In an odd way, however, certain types of job gravitated, as if of their own volition, toward one man. Wrexall's knowledge of blackmail was the most exhaustive at Scotland Yard. He had that sense of "smell." Now, he had picked out something which might be significant from a series of reports covering several months, from different divisions. Where another man might have read these reports a hundred times and seen nothing in them, Wrexall had picked out two things:

A respected suburban solicitor had committed suicide six months ago, but his affairs were in order; the only surprise was that his estate had been much smaller than expected. Nothing at all was missing from clients' funds. The police investigation, prior to the inquest at which the verdict had been suicide while temporarily insane, showed that he had changed his daily habits a great deal during the past two years, had frequently left his office in charge of a junior partner and, it was believed, had "gone racing"; that was the official explanation of the missing private fortune and the fact that he had left an elderly wife unprovided for.

Two months later, in another London suburb, the manager of a large branch of one of the joint stock banks had been killed in an accident. The police had suspected suicide, but had not been able to establish it, and the verdict had at least been a comfort to his widow and two children. They had little else to comfort them, for a personal estate, known at one time to have been worth nearly thirty thousand pounds, had vanished. There was no certainty about the way in which the loss had been made, but gambling was suspected.

Wrexall, studying these, had seen the similarity of social position, suicide and suspected suicide, and a small fortune lost either unaccountably or in a way which was surprising when one considered the character of the dead man.

"Just made me wonder whether everything was what it looked like, George," Wrexall had said. He had a mane of iron-gray hair and a most impressive manner. "You know what I'm like, nose as long as a snorkel device. So I put young Chambers onto finding out who the solicitor had placed his bets with. Couldn't find anyone, local or in the West End. In fact, I'm pretty sure he didn't have an account with any bookie. Then I checked the racecourses, finding out the days that the chap had taken out big cash sums. Most of them coincided with race days near London, and I tried to find a bookie who'd taken big bets with the solicitor. Couldn't. In fact there weren't any big cash bets on any of those days. Funny, eh?"

Gideon had agreed that it was funny.

"Now if these two chaps were paying out money under pressure and didn't want to show it, they'd fake a reason, wouldn't they?" said Wrexall. "But I don't like to think that anyone's managed to drive chaps like them to suicide, as well as make things tough for their families. So I've been keeping my eyes open, and this morning there's an interesting little report in from Guildford. Outside our ground, I know, but very interesting. Accountant, this time, tried to commit suicide. Inherited twenty-five thousand quid four years ago, lived a normal married life as far as we can see—and he's almost on his beam ends. It's no use me ringing up Guildford or the Surrey boys, but if you'd have a word with the A.C. and persuade him that it might be worth looking at, he could lay it on with the Chief Constable of Surrey, and—"

"You could have a few nice, cozy days in the country," Gideon had grinned. "Okay, Tim, I'll tell him it's too good to miss. That worth the money you'll pay for the lunch?"

"Don't know what I'd do without you," Wrexall had said. "Glad to sit and watch you eat, anyway. I never could tell where you put it all."

They went back to the Yard at a leisurely pace, Gideon still glowing from the smooth morning, and because so much had gone right; his regret about the way the Primrose Girl case was turning was almost forgotten. He was even philosophic about Syd's continued absence; had the boy been killed, they would probably have found the body by now; he'd turn up. He had no suspicion of what kind of news would greet him until he opened the door and Lemaitre burst out:

"George, Benson's got his wife's beau! Vitriol. Horrible job, hospital case. And Abbott caught some, too."

Gideon stood quite still, with the door open. He felt the old, crushing weight coming down on him again, and when he moved it was more slowly than usual. He closed the door, and the lock snapped. He stood with his back to it, massive and, in that mood, almost frightening.

"How bad's Small?"

"Side of his face and one eye," Lemaitre said.

"Abbott?"

"Left hand only, as far as I can gather; he's not a hospital case, anyhow—on his way here now."

"Benson?"

"A kid did the job."

Gideon almost groaned, "Not young Syd."

"Dunno," said Lemaitre.

Wrexall's suspicions, Cummings and his worry, the Rose family, the newspaper reports—all of these things vanished from Gideon's mind. He walked to his desk, and it was as if he were walking through shadows, not through bright shafts of sunlight which struck and brightened the wall behind his desk. He sat down slowly, loosened his collar and tie, and took out his pipe. He began to finger the roughened surface.

Then, he made himself say, "Anything else in?"

"Not much," answered Lemaitre. "They caught a shop-lifter at Marridge's. He made a dash for it, and caused a bit of panic, then fell down the stairs and broke his leg. Two smash-and-grabs—one in Soho, one near Marble Arch, nothing much gone. Two—"

"Sure Abbott's not badly hurt?"

"Yes."

"Mrs. Benson know about this?"

"Bound to. Happened just outside the shop."

Then, two telephones rang at the same moment. Lemaitre snatched his up; Gideon took his more slowly and raised it as slowly to his ear. "Gideon." He heard Lemaitre say something in his laconic way, but wasn't sure what it was. He could see Arthur Small as if he were here in the office: earnest, faithful, well-preserved, well-groomed, with his pale, regular features, his horn-rimmed glasses.

Glasses?

"Detective Officer Abbott is in the building, sir, would you like to see him?"

"Yes. Right away. Send him up."

"Thank you, sir."

Gideon started to fill the bowl of his pipe, and to find that his mind began to thaw out. He was able to remind himself that this might be the most important but it wasn't the only job on his plate, and he must not allow it to obsess him, even for a few minutes. Then, he realized that in fact it had obsessed him. The awful, hideous mask of failure—such failure that it was possible for a man whom they were "protecting" to be disfigured in this way—was one of the most bitter things he had ever had to face. It undid all the good of last night; of this morning. The Press, the Home Office, the Assistant Commissioner, every man and woman at Scotland Yard might make excuses; but he, Gideon, felt just one thing: it should never have happened and it was his fault that it had. He'd met young Abbott in the lift, formed a good opinion of him, and given him a job which should have been handled by a man with much more experience. The whole world would call that nonsense, but he, Gideon, knew the simple truth.

It was a heavy weight, bearing hard upon him.

There was a tap at the door.

"Come in," he called.

Lemaitre was still talking, but was glancing toward the door as it opened, and Abbott came in. He didn't look very good; his face had lost that healthy glow, in spite of the tan, and Gideon knew that he was suffering from shock; he ought to stay away for a day or so. His right hand was bandaged, and there was a patch of sticking plaster on his right cheek, about an inch from his eye. He kept himself erect with an obvious effort.

What the hell was his Christian name?

Ah: Michael.

He looked as if he expected Gideon to breathe fire.

"Hallo, Mike," Gideon said quietly, "come and sit down." He didn't overdo it, but just waved to a chair, and then pushed a pack of cigarettes across the desk. "Glad to see you didn't come out of it too badly."

Abbott just sat there, his shoulders less square, now, the dejection a physical as well as a mental thing. He didn't take a cigarette. He didn't look round. He managed to meet Gideon's gaze, and that was all. Here was a man who could be broken for life; moments like this condemned men, like patient old Jefferson, to a life in which the highest possible ambition was a sergeant's pension.

"What time did it happen?" asked Gideon. If he could once start the man talking . . .

His telephone bell rang.

"Blast the blurry thing," he said, and picked it up more quickly than usual. "Matches?" He tossed a big box across the desk, and it slid off. Abbott had to bend down to pick it up and, with the matches in his hand, he seemed to lose some of the tension, and then picked up the cigarettes. "Gideon here," said Gideon; "switch all calls through to Chief Inspector Lemaitre until . . . *what?*"

He listened so intently that Abbott, the cigarette now between his lips, looked at him almost eagerly. So did Lemaitre who got up and came across.

Then:

"Thank God for that," breathed Gideon. "Eh . . . Yes, he's with me now . . . Not badly hurt, seems to have done a good job . . . Oh, fine. Fine. Thanks, sir."

He rang off and was smiling; not the broad, homely smile which made him so likable and attractive to many people, but a smile which had a kind of glow about it; in a woman, it would have been radiant. It was the last thing that either Lemaitre or Abbott had dreamed of seeing, and it must have done Abbott more good than anything else could have.

"That was the A.C.," he said. "Young Syd's been found. He's not hurt. Been hiding out with Charlie Mulliver, kind of blurry fool thing Charlie would do, harbor him when he knew we were on the lookout for him. Wouldn't I like to put him inside! And Small won't lose the sight of his right eye, after all; he'll have a scar on the side of his face, up round the temple, that's about all. Lem, ring the shop and tell Mrs. Benson, and if she's not in, ring the Division and ask them to tell her—that's if she doesn't know already." Gideon put his pipe to his lips. "Well, things aren't always as black as they seem, Mike," he said to Abbott. "Feel better?"

Abbott gulped; when he spoke his voice was pitched higher than usual.

"Can't alter the fact that I ought to have stopped the Benson kid from getting away, and I ought to have stopped the other kid from throwing that acid, too. Didn't dream of anything coming from him. He's a half-wit near as damnit, I've often seen him hanging about. When I start thinking, I know that Benson must have found a way to get in touch with him, but at the time he was just a kid to be sorry for. You know."

"I know," Gideon said. "Half-wit, is he?"

"Well known round there, too," said Abbott. Now his voice was more normal, as if his throat had been oiled, but he was speaking very quickly. "Named Simon, people call him Si, but whether that's from Simple Simon I don't know. It's a crying shame, a boy like that ought to be in a home, but he even goes to school! He's at the G5 Division now, there's a doctor with him. They think we'll frighten the wits out of him if we bring him here. But even if he knows who told him to do it, there's no way we can make sure that he tells us."

"We can try," Gideon said. "Just what happened?"

Abbott told him; and before the recital was finished, he was talking at normal speed and in his normal voice.

Gideon sent him home.

Gideon did not labor the obvious fact: that Benson had managed to get in touch with the half-wit, and to give him instructions—almost certainly through a third party.

Who?

The dozens of friends and acquaintances with whom Benson might have got in touch would have to be picked up now, and a full-scale interrogation begun. The movements of the hapless vitriol thrower had to be traced. Given the breaks, none of it should take long; but one fact stood out: Benson had headed for London for vengeance. His wife would be in greater terror than ever; so would his daughter. The one good thing was that young Syd was back.

Was it so good?

Gideon got his mind very clear on what had happened, and what he was going to ask the boy—and say to Mulliver.

The man who had sheltered the boy ran a doss house near the docks; beds at a shilling a night, bring your own food, kill your own rats, find your own lice. It was a place that ought to be closed up on grounds of unsanitary conditions, yet by some miracle it managed to meet all the London County Council rules and regulations. Mulliver, a middle-aged wreck of a man, had a good reputation for helping lame dogs, and he got on well with the police. He wasn't a squealer; as far as was known, he wasn't a crook, either.

Had he let young Syd stay with him out of the goodness of his heart, or under some kind of pressure?

From Benson, for instance . . .

That was just a guess; but it was an accurate guess.

Even if he soon became certain of its accuracy, there still lay upon Gideon the burden of proof.

He cleared up everything on his desk and, about half past three, went to the G5 Division. First, he wanted to see the half-wit, to find out what the Divisional people had done; then he wanted to talk to Charlie Mulliver; next, to young Syd.

One thing was certain: as this news spread, and by now it would have reached every Division, every sub-division, every plain-clothes man and every man on the beat in the whole of the London area, the whole of the Metropolitan Police would be geared to a pitch which it reached only now and again.

Every man would feel it his personal responsibility to make sure that Benson was caught before he could harm his wife or her children.

Gideon felt that the responsibility was all his.

Mulliver swore that young Syd had come to him, pleading to be allowed to hide.

"And where was the harm?" the doss-house keeper almost whined. "I couldn't see any, Mr. Gideon, honest I couldn't."

He didn't change his story, but there was much he could have told.

17 . Father and Son

There was just one thing about Charlie Mulliver which the police did not know, and which Syd Benson did.

He was a murderer.

He was not a natural killer, in the way that Benson was. In fact he still had a compassion for his fellow men which, in view of the people he mixed with over the years, was quite surprising. If a man really needed a bed and a cup of tea and a hunk of bread, and couldn't pay for it he would get it at Charlie's; a great many people went to his "hotel" in preference to the Salvation Army Hostel or the Y.M.C.A. or any of the other do-good places in the East End of London.

But Charlie Mulliver had killed his wife.

That was five years ago, and the case had long since been left high on the archives of the Yard, not as un-solvable, but as unsolved or pending. Mulliver's wife, in the common phrase, had been no better than she ought to be. At one time she had helped to run the doss house, looking after a women's section, as well as assisting on the other side. She had bestowed her favors too liberally, and in a quarrel Charlie had killed her. At the time, he had been drunk; at the time he had meant only to disfigure her; but if he were ever caught for the job he would certainly be jailed for life.

Syd Benson was the only man who knew who had killed her. Syd had helped to put the body in the Thames. And the police, knowing her habits, had not really been surprised when they had taken it out. They had questioned Mulliver, of course; and at one time the doss-house keeper had seemed the most likely suspect, but they had reckoned without the organizing genius of Benson. Having set out to fool the police for Mulliver's sake, Benson had succeeded brilliantly, by fixing an alibi at third hand and in a way which the police had never seriously questioned.

Mulliver had been a widower for five years, and all that time had known that one day Benson would want something in return for his help and his silence. There was nothing that Mulliver wouldn't do, to drive away even the thought of paying for his wife's murder.

Benson was not only clever and shrewd, but was also a sound judge of human nature. He knew that Mulliver would do whatever he was told, no matter how serious a crime. Like nine criminals out of every ten, Mulliver would feel that whatever he did, he would avoid being found out. All he had to do was pay his debt to Benson; after that, he would have nothing to worry about.

If Mulliver refused to obey Benson however, Benson would make sure that police would know all about the murder of his wife.

So Mulliver really had no choice.

And his life had been spent in the worst part of the East End, rubbing shoulders with vice and crime, with all that was worst as well as some of the things that were best in human nature. No one could have remained a saint for long while surrounded by that atmosphere, and Charlie Mulliver had been soaked in it for forty-odd years; but, the murder apart, he was not a criminal. It was not so much that he disapproved of crime as that he liked to keep himself safe from its consequences. It worked, too; he was trusted by the crooks and tolerated by the police.

Subconsciously, the gift of compassion in Charlie Mulliver was perhaps a form of self-defense. It paid off to have a heart. But he became so used to violence and crime at second hand that little shocked him. Among the hundreds of down-and-outs, drunks, men wounded in fights, sailors, Negroes, lascars, half-breeds and white men of all nationalities who passed through the doss house, dozens were badly scarred by acid, knife or razor. Scars were commonplace. So when Charlie had been told to brief Simon called Si to throw vitriol into Arthur Small's face, Charlie Mulliver had not revolted against the idea; he knew dozens of people whose faces and bodies were scarred by vitriol; and they'd lived through it. And above all things he had to ingratiate himself with Benson. He'd made a start when he had first learned that Benson was out, by telephoning his wife's boy friend.

Lilies or roses?—that would make Benson laugh!

Cunningly, Mulliver did the vitriol job through a third party, so that Simple Si could not possibly give him away to the police. The man the lad could have given away was now well out in the English Channel, on his way to Australia as a stoker on a small tramp steamer, and there was no danger from him either. So Mulliver felt quite safe. If he was at all uneasy, it was that he had kept young Syd here, but he'd received the order from Benson, and he hadn't seriously thought of refusing to obey. He had known of a dozen places where he could hide the boy, and had decided that the safest was in the doss house—in one of the tiny little private rooms where he lived himself. There had been no trouble at all with young Syd when he'd told him that it was his father's instructions.

All Syd wanted was to see his father.

And on the morning of the fifth day, the morning after Jingo Smith's capture, the morning after Gideon had become a hero, the morning which had gone so well, young Syd Benson had met his father for the first time in four years.

Young Syd hadn't realized what was going to happen. Mulliver hadn't warned him, but Benson had arrived in London the previous night. He had several days' stubble on his lean face, and looked rough and vicious. Freddy Tisdale was still with him. They had come in on a big truck from Birmingham; the journey had been arranged by Benson's Birmingham friends, and they had arrived in the darkness of early morning. They hadn't gone to the doss house but had been hiding inside big barrels in an empty warehouse not far from the spot where Jingo Smith had made his attempt to blow himself and others sky-high.

It was more an oil dump than a warehouse, not far from Charlie Mulliver's place. It was easy for Benson and Tisdale to get across roofs to the doss house and eat, but at the slightest warning they could go back to the warehouse. It was true that if the police searched the doss house they might find evidence that Benson and Tisdale had been there, but to take all reasonable precautions against that, whenever they were there, they wore cotton gloves and so made sure they didn't leave prints.

The doss house emptied during the day; from ten o'clock until five or six in the evening, there was no one there except Mulliver, a drab who did some of the cleaning for him, and occasional visitors.

It was not until the night guests had departed that Mulliver had gone in to see young Syd and said with that tone of simulated kindliness,

"Your Dad wants to see you, Syd. Coming?"

Young Syd Benson, unable to realize that he was actually looking upon his father in the flesh, stood on the threshold of the dingy little room where Benson and Tisdale spent some of their time. Tisdale was over at the warehouse; Benson wanted to see his son alone. Mulliver gave the boy a push and sent him further into the room, then backed out and closed the door. He kept near it, however, ready to raise the alarm if anyone arrived unexpectedly.

Father and son stood looking at each other.

Young Syd just saw a dream; a dream which had become real for a few minutes on the television, only to fade. Now it was back. The black stubble made no difference; the thin face made little; the sharp lines at the side of the mouth meant nothing to him. The living part of his father's face was in those pale eyes.

Benson's black stubble made them look much brighter and lighter even than they were. Shimmering. They were fine eyes, too; and the man who stood there, the dream which had come to life, was striking to look at. With his chiseled chin and his sharp nose and the deep eye-sockets, Benson was handsome in a kind of piratical way.

The odd thing was that they stood so still for a long time.

Young Syd was just numbed; unbelieving; and yet rising toward a tremendous exaltation.

Benson did not feel like that, but he felt an emotion which he had never experienced before: a kind of pride in his son, a kind of satisfaction that here in front of him was a chip off the old block. No one could doubt that he was face to face with his own flesh and blood.

"Hallo, boyo," Benson said very slowly. He clenched his right fist as he moved forward, and pressed the knuckles against the other pointed chin. Young Syd didn't give ground, even when Benson increased the pressure so that it must have hurt. Then: "How do you like seeing your Dad again, boyo;" Benson asked in that clipped, grating voice, and he looked almost savagely into his son's eyes.

"It's the only thing I've wanted for a long time," young Syd breathed.

Benson took his hand away from the child's jaw and gripped his shoulder. His finger bit deeply, but Syd did not flinch. He shook his son two or three times, making him sway forward and backward, but nothing altered the way that young Syd looked at him, with a light that was almost of veneration in his eyes.

"Well, I don't mind getting a look at you again," Benson said, and let the boy go. "You all right? They been looking after you?"

"Yeh," said young Syd.

"If they haven't, you just tell me."

"I'm okay," young Syd said firmly.

"Sure, you look okay to me," his father said, and grinned. "Didn't expect me to get out of jug, did you?"

"Yes, I did," said Syd flatly.

Benson exclaimed: "What's that?"

"Course I expected you to get out! I used to tell the other chaps that you wouldn't stay in jug all that time," boasted Syd, and his eyes were still radiant. "I was right, wasn't I?"

"You knew a thing or two," agreed Benson, and his eyes seemed to soften. "Well, I'll tell you another thing, boyo. I'm not going to let them take me back."

"I bet you're not!"

"Now I'm out, I'm out for keeps," Benson said, and his eyes narrowed, his voice dropped. "Sometimes to get the things you want you have to do things you don't like, Syd. Get me? You heard about that cove in the car park, up in Millways?"

Syd gulped, and nodded.

"Well, do you know what he was going to do? He was going to shop me, Syd, that's what he was going to do. Couldn't let that happen, could I?"

Syd gritted his teeth and shook his head.

It wasn't because he felt any sense of horror or reproach; it was because the emotion which he had held in check, unkowingly, was beginning to force itself to the surface. Tears stung his eyes; and it was a long, long time since he had cried. He stood there, jaws working, teeth gritting together, and tears glistening in those eyes which were so much like his father's. Benson stopped speaking. He did not understand this behavior at first, and his manner changed; he was resentful, wary. Then, before he could do anything to stop it, the boy had flung himself forward and crushed himself against him, crying:

"Dad, oh Dad, Dad, Dad!"

Benson stood quite still, feeling the pressure of the taut young body, the hardness of his son's head on his chin, the grip of his son's arms round him. He heard the choking, sobbing cries. He felt something he had never known before, something which had not even been within his understanding. His own eyes felt the sting of sharp, unfamiliar emotion—something that he hadn't felt when he had been sentenced, that he hadn't felt for a single moment while he had been at Millways.

The boy began to shiver.

Gradually, he went still.

Benson eased him away, and said with a rough kindliness which was quite foreign to him: "Now take it easy, kid, you'll be all right. Just take it easy."

They waited there, feeling different now, Syd sniffing and rubbing the sleeve of his jersey across his eyes and nose, Benson watching him with that new-found pride and a fierce sense of complete possession. It was not really long, but to them it seemed a long time before he spoke.

"So that's okay, now forget it, see. You want to know something? I've got a plan to get out of the country, go somewhere the bloody coppers can't get me."

"You—you have?"

"Sure. South America. You heard of South America?"

Young Syd, still sniffing and still not able to trust himself to speak properly, just managed to nod.

"Well, that's where I'm going. A pal of mine can fix me up on a ship; I'm going as a member of the crew, see. False name and all that, and I don't need no passport. As soon as I'm three miles outside the British waters, I'm free as the air, see. The captain's in the know, but he's a foreigner and he's getting well paid for it, so it's okay."

"That—that's good," Syd said.

Benson thrust out a hand, put his forefinger under the boy's chin, and forced his head back. The eyes were not yet competely free from tears, and were red and swollen.

"Say, what's this? Don't you want me to go?"

"Oh, yeh, course I do!"

"You didn't sound exactly enthusiastic."

Syd didn't try to look away, but said clearly, "I won't see you again for a long time, will I?"

Benson began to grin again; then he relaxed properly for the first time, took out a packet of cigarettes, lit one, and flicked the match across the little, shadowy room.

"So that's the trouble, is it? Don't want to lose me again, eh? Well, you needn't, boyo. They can try to separate father and son, but we know a way of putting that right, don't we? You want to know something? There's just one little job you've got to do for me, and then we'll get aboard this ship together. You come as a cabin boy, like they did in the old days. Okay?"

Syd said gaspingly, "Can—can I really?"

"Think I'd lie to my own flesh and blood? Sure, you can come, I'll fix it. But don't forget that job you've got to do first, will you?"

"Just tell me what it is, and I'll do it!"

"That's the boy." Now, Benson's expression changed again, and the look in his eyes was hard and calculating; much as it had been when he had talked with Freddy Tisdale up in the furnished house in Millways. He stared for a long time, until the child began to shift his feet, uneasy and unsure of himself. "Okay, let's talk," Benson said abruptly. "How's your ma?"

"She—she's okay."

"She never talk about me?"

"Not—not much."

"She try to turn you against me?"

"No," said young Syd, because it did not occur to him that his father might want him to lie. "She only talks about you if—well, if something happens to remind her. Like the escape from the prison. That—Dad, it was your idea, wasn't it?"

"Mine and no one else's," Benson boasted.

"I knew it was! I told everybody at school it was you, and there was a chap named Lewis, he said it was Jingo Smith. I didn't half sock him one!"

"That's the ticket," Benson said, with deep satisfaction. "Anyone says anything you don't like, sock him one. It was me who thought up that escape, and don't you forget it. And I'll get the two of us on that ship going to South America, don't you forget that, either. Your ma get those headaches like she used to?"

"Sometimes."

"Still take aspirins?"

"Yes." Syd looked puzzled, but didn't ask a question.

"Just goes on the same way, eh? This guy she's got living with her, you like him?"

"I—I don't know who you mean?"

"This Small, Art Small." Benson was impatient.

"Oh, him," said Syd disparagingly. "He don't live at home, but he comes round most nights, so he might just as well. If he don't come home, she goes out with him to the pictures or somewhere."

"Like him?"

Syd answered slowly, as if he hadn't given the matter any thought at all: "Well, no, not exactly."

"Okay, forget him. What about your sister? She okay?"

"Oh, yeh, she's fine."

"Get on all right with you, does she?"

"She's okay," Syd said; "she's like anyone else's sister; you know what sisters are like."

Benson grinned.

"That's where you're wrong, son, I never had a sister. Never had a ma or a pa, either. Orphan brat, that's what I was. Had to fend for myself from the time I was nine, and don't you forget it. That's how I came to know the best way to look after Number One. Now, listen to me, boyo. You're going back home, see. You're not to tell your ma or anyone else you've seen me. Just say you've been holding out in Charlie Mulliver's place, the police won't worry much about Charlie. Just go home and be yourself, see. Don't talk about me to anyone, just be yourself, just look as if you knew you was going to stay there for the rest of your life. You've gone back because you didn't see the pay-off for you if you stayed away. Got all that, Syd?"

The boy was eager.

"Yeh!"

"That's fine. And listen. You say your ma still gets those headaches and takes aspirins?"

"Like I told you."

"That's fine. Well, I'm going to give you some special aspirin tablets, boyo, and you're going to look after them until you get back. First time your ma says she wants an aspirin, you go and get them for her, see, and you give her one of the tablets I'm going to give you. Got that? One or two, makes no odds, but she's to have them instead of the aspirins."

Syd, his eagerness slightly dulled by a kind of bewilderment, asked slowly,

"I can do that, okay, but why? Are they better than ordinary aspirins?"

"I'll say they are, son," said Benson; and now his expression was wholly evil, hard, vicious, in spite of the fact that his lips were twisted into a smile. "They're tons better. She'll go right off to sleep, see, and then you can sneak out of the house and come right back here to me. She just won't hear you, that's a fact. We'll get off on that ship for South America right away, then. You understand?"

The boy's eyes held a light which they had never shown before. He could not speak, could only nod. When his father held out a little bottle in which were two white tablets which looked like aspirins, he took the bottle and put it in his pocket without saying a word. He was swamped by emotion again, but not so helplessly as before, and this time he forced it back by his own efforts.

Benson gripped his shoulder with that same painful tightness.

"Okay, boyo?"

"Sure."

"That's fine," said Benson, but he didn't relax his grip. "Now listen, son. The police will ask you a lot of questions, you know what these perishing dicks are like. So they ask you questions. You don't tell them a thing. You didn't see me, you haven't heard from home, you just stayed at Charlie's place, until you realized there was no future in it. Understand?" Now his grip was really painful, and the boy drew in his breath but made no attempt to get clear. "Listen to me, boyo, if you so much as whisper that you've seen me, that trip's off, see. I won't wait for you, I'll go on me own. Understand?"

"I wouldn't tell them if they killed me," young Syd said.

18 . Benson Talks

Benson stayed at Charlie Mulliver's place for an hour after his son had gone, and then slipped along an alley and over some roofs to the warehouse, using a window which appeared to be locked from the outside, but had been rigged so that it could open easily. He had a bag with a packet of food, four bottles of beer, cigarettes, matches, chocolates, and a pack of playing cards. He was through the window in a moment, and stood by it, listening intently for several seconds; he heard no sound of anyone approaching.

He turned round.

There was a strong smell of petrol in the warehouse; thousands of gallons of petrol in forty-gallon metal drums were stored here. There were other fuel oils, too; the place would become a ready-made incinerator if a naked flame got near any of the oils. It was dark and gloomy except near the window, yet Benson did not use his flashlight. He picked his way over the metal drums, kicking against one now and again so that it gave off a deep booming note, but the window was closed and the warehouse was almost soundproof.

He reached a doorway which led to a pair of wooden steps, a big, square freight lift with open ironwork gates, which led to the floors above. He used the stairs and, as he neared the first landing, heard a whisper of sound. He tapped three times on the wooden handrail, and immediately the handrail quivered from Freddy Tisdale's responding taps. Then Freddy called softly:

"Everything okay?"

"Everything's fine."

"Got some grub?"

"Plenty."

Freddy said, "And can I use it!" He was at the first landing, and now he turned away, in the gloom, toward a little room which had once been used as an office but had not been needed for that purpose for a long time. On the floor along two sides of the walls were bundles of rags, making rough mattresses, and there were blankets for the men to throw over themselves at night. There was a small table, two packing cases to sit on, a candle in the neck of a beer bottle, and a safety lamp. The only light came from a small, frosted glass window set very high in the wall, and they lived here in a state of almost perpetual gloom.

Benson put the food on the table. Freddy tore at it, then opened a bottle of beer and tossed it down his throat; the gurgling seemd very loud. Looking at him, Benson saw the line of his neck, almost straight from his breastbones to the tip of his chin. A funny thought occurred to Benson, then: that a knife laid against that throat would make the flesh twang like tightly stretched wire being cut.

Freddy gasped as he put the bottle down.

"That's better," he said thickly; "plenty more where it came from?"

"Enough," said Benson.

They ate; they lit cigarettes; and they sat against the walls, facing each other. Freddy started several different subjects of conversation, but they all fell flat. Then he asked if Benson had seen the kid.

"Sure," Benson said.

"He okay?"

"He's fine," said Benson, "he's the way I like him." There was a new, vibrant note in his voice, a depth of feeling different from anything which Freddy Tisdale had heard before. In spite of the gloom, he could see the way Benson's eyes glistened, and he sensed something of what was going on in the other man's mind.

Then Benson began to talk.

He had never talked so freely as this about any subject; just uttered a word or the clipped sentences, and lapsed into long periods of silence. Now he talked as if whisky had loosened his tongue, but there was no whisky on his breath, there was just the spirit of that boy. He talked, not knowing it, with all the pent-up love that he felt for his son, and all he had ever dreamed for him, all that had lain buried so long in his subconscious mind now came out and took possession of him.

And Freddy Tisdale listened, fascinated at first.

At last, Benson stopped. He picked up a bottle of beer,

smacked it sharply against the table and knocked the neck off, and then put it to his lips, as if it did not occur to him that the broken glass would cut him.

He drank deeply.

"That's the way it goes," he said clearly. "That boy's a chip off the old block, and no mistake. Give him ten years and he'll be as good as his father. That boy's got a future, Freddy, you can take it from me. Wouldn't I like to have seen him growing up, instead of letting that—"

He broke off.

He gave the twisted, hateful smile.

"Well, she's got hers," he said.

He stopped speaking, put a cigarette to his lips and then lit it. He watched the match burn out, unwinking. He did not appear to notice that Freddy had gone very still and quiet. Freddy was staring at him; and after a while Benson looked round, saw that, and asked in a harsh voice,

"Seen enough?"

"Syd," said Freddy, and gulped and broke off. Now Benson sat there, with the empty beer bottle in his hand, and the broken neck with its jagged edges pointing toward Freddy; it had once been his favorite form of weapon.

"What's biting you?"

Freddy said, "Syd, you—you haven't been there and killed her?"

Benson stared in turn, and then let his arm fall; he banged the thick end of the bottle on the table and began to laugh. The fact that he laughed aloud the first time since they had broken out of prison told Freddy a great deal about the state of his nerves: how tense they were and how easy it might be to break them.

"Strike me," he said at last, "what do you think I am? Go and see the old So-and-so? Me? With Gideon and half the flippin' police on the doorstep? Have some sense, Freddy boy, have some sense!"

"But you said—"

"I said she's got hers, and that's what I meant," Benson told him, "and I gave it to her. But not the way you think, son, not the way anyone thinks. Like to know how I fixed it?" He laughed again, but this time there was an edge to the laughter, and it came out slowly, as if he were not quite sure that it was wise to laugh or to talk. Abruptly: "The kid'll fix it."

Freddy caught his breath.

"Young Syd?"

"Any complaint?"

"You can't trust a kid like that to croak his own mother; even if he was pleased to see you, he—"

Benson said, "Stow it. He was pleased to see me all right; and if I'd asked him, he'd have fixed her. But he's only a kid, ain't he? Think I'd want a kid to know he was going to do a thing like that? Not bloody likely! He's going to give her some aspirins, that's all, just a coupla aspirins. He won't know what's happened to her. Why, the way these doctors and psychologists work these days they won't even tell him what happened, they'll just ask him where he got the aspirins from, that's all—even if they get round to that. Let me tell you something, Freddy. They're soft about kids, these days. The worst that can happen to him is a few years in Borstal, and that won't hurt him. It could do him a hell of a lot of good, the same way as it did me. Syd'll be okay. But Ruby'll know what it's like to be all twisted up inside before those aspirins have finished doing their job. What with her boy friend's face all burned off him, and—"

He broke off again.

Freddy said, in a strangely weak voice, "You know what you want, Syd, don't you?"

"And I get it."

Silence followed, and lasted for a long time. It was uneasy; sullen. The broken bottle stood on the table between them, the right way up; in Benson's pocket was the poultry knife. About them was the gloom of the dingy office, and below-stairs the barrels of petrol and other oils, the bare walls with the great hanging cobwebs, the spiders, the rats, the bats. Outside, just across the alley, was the little window of Charlie Mulliver's doss house, and beyond that the East End and Muskett Street—where Ruby Benson stood talking, not knowing, then, what was going to happen to Art Small that lunchtime.

Then, Freddy said, "Syd, you got everything laid on for that ship?"

"I told you, didn't I?"

"Can't go wrong. The captain's drunk half the time, and he's brought so much snow into the country he daren't refuse me a passage—the five hundred each wasn't for him, it was to grease a lot of palms. Didn't anyone tell you that palms want greasing sometimes?"

Freddy forced a smile. "As if I didn't know."

"You know. I'll tell you what," went on Benson. He became expansive again, sitting back with his shoulders and his head against the wall, and a dreamy smile on his face; it touched him with the gentleness of what might have been. "We'll have a two-berth cabin on board, see? We'll ship as crew, but as soon as we're out at sea we'll be treated like favored passengers—the only two, in the bargain. The ship's carrying machine parts, and couldn't be cleaner. We'll live like fighting cocks, that's what we'll do, deck chairs and sunshine all day long, just a couple of bucks out on the sea voyage for the sake of their health. And when we get to Buenos Aires, o-kay! We find ourselves something to do. We find ourselves a couple of señoritas, too. You remember that skirt we used to know, back along? Spanish, she was, and—oh, boy!"

He stopped.

He didn't go on again, this time, but stayed there with the half-smile on his lips, his eyes nearly closed, just able to see Freddy between his lashes. Soon, with his eyes closed firmly, he looked as if he were asleep, breathing smoothly and without the slightest hint of a snore—a compact, handsome man with that black stubble and the deep lines of suffering and hardship at his mouth.

Freddy closed his eyes, too, but kept opening them again. Every now and again his lips tightened, and he seemed to be looking at Benson for something that he wasn't very sure about, something he couldn't be sure was there. He could not settle to a book, although there were several old paper-backed Westerns here.

Ruby Benson was back at Muskett Street.

A relief manager had been sent to the dress shop in the Mile End Road as soon as the news of the attack on Arthur Small had been reported. He had sent Ruby home at once, full of reassurance and understanding; she wasn't to worry, she was to stay away from business until this period of anxiety was over; she needn't have a care in the world. There was no need for him to provide an escort, for four policemen were now outside the shop; and wherever one looked, on the way from the Mile End Road to Muskett Street, it seemed as if there was a policeman. In fact there were three in Muskett Street, and two of them went into the little house and looked in every room before Ruby was allowed to go in. That was in spite of the fact that the house had been under surveillance day and night for nearly five days.

That had been at two o'clock.

Liz had been on her way back to school, and Ruby hadn't tried to get her back.

At a quarter past two, a policeman came hurrying across the road, and she saw him through the front-room window. She was in there, hardly knowing what she was doing, wishing that she was with Art Small, knowing it would be no use waiting at the hospital. He might lose his sight, and he might die. She did not think consciously of her husband; she was obsessed by anxiety for the man who had brought so much brightness into her life.

Then the policeman outside knocked sharply.

Ruby got up, hesitated, and moved slowly toward the passage, then toward the front door. She knew that this could mean trouble, and it could also mean good news. She felt a sharp pain at her side as she thought of that, and pressed a hand against her aching head.

She had never had a worse headache.

It showed in her glassy eyes and in the twitching nerves at the corners of her eyes. The bang at the front door seemed to go right through her, making the pain much worse. Then she managed to make herself step forward, and opened the door.

The middle-aged policeman standing on the doorstep looked really excited.

Had the police caught *him*? Hope flared.

"Your boy's okay, Mrs. Benson," the policeman said quickly. "He's on his way here now, just turned the corner." His eagerness faded when he saw Ruby's expression and guessed at the pain she felt, but he went on: "Hope I'm not talking out of turn, but mind if I suggest something?"

"Syd's coming back? Young Syd?" Ruby felt a sudden relief, a kind of gladness. So her son could ease the pressure of her despair.

"Nearly here now, Mrs. Benson," the policeman said, "and if you'll take a tip from me you won't go for him too much for running away. Treat him gently now, and it might make all the difference."

She looked as if she hadn't heard a word.

"And he isn't hurt?"

"No," said the policeman, "he's all right, and—" He

broke off, giving up his well-intentioned effort, and he watched her as she pushed past him, into the street. Her expression was very different from anything he had expected. Her eyes didn't glow, but there was no anger in them, and for the first time he realized what a good-looking girl Mrs. Benson must have been when she was young.

She stared along the street.

Young Syd was coming toward her, at the side of a plain-clothes man. His head was held high, and he walked defiantly. Ruby caught her breath, for he looked so like big Syd when she had first met him; as if he were prepared to look the world in the face, and nothing could keep him down.

She found herself hurrying.

"Syd, oh, Syd . . ."

He didn't break into a run. He did nothing to suggest that he was pleased to see her. When she bent down and took him in her arms, he didn't yield, as once he had, but kept his body stiff and aloof. She realized that, and it marred the relief of his return. She realized—or told herself that she did—that it would be a long time before she won his confidence again, that she would have to be very, very careful about the way she treated him.

She took him in.

"What's the matter, Mum?" he asked. "You got a headache?"

She wondered if he cared whether she had a headache or not, and couldn't quite understand the sharpness in his voice.

"A bit of one," she said.

"I'll get you an aspirin, I know where . . ."

"I took two just before you came in," Ruby said; "I won't take any more yet, Syd. Syd, where—" She checked herself; questions could come later, just now she had to try to win him over. For although she did not know where he had been, she realized that he had really gone chasing after his dream—that if he could have found him, he would have run off to see his father. "Are you hungry, Syd?" she asked quietly. "What would you like to eat?"

At half past four, Liz arrived, bursting into the house and hugging Syd.

At twenty to five, Gideon arrived.

19 . The Truth?

Gideon had come straight from Charlie Mulliver, and he was a long way from certain that Charlie had told the simple truth. There was something worrying Charlie, and it might easily have to do with young Syd. Gideon hadn't said or done anything to suggest that he was not satisfied that all Charlie had done was to give the runaway shelter, but after he had left he had called the Yard on his walkie-talkie radio.

"Give me Chief Inspector Lemaitre . . .

"Lem, George here. Have a word with the Division and tell them to check on Charlie Mulliver's place, will you? Don't give themselves away more than they can help, but just check who's been in and out of there lately."

"You got something, George?"

"Could have," said Gideon, and rang off.

Ten minutes later, he was entering the little house in Muskett Street. He had the latest report from the hospital about Arthur Small, and it was reasonably good; he expected Ruby to make difficulties when he started to question the boy, but whether she liked it or not, that had to be done.

The sight of half a dozen policemen in the street depressed him; it should not be necessary to have so many; the attack on Small had put the breeze up all of them; not excluding Commander Gideon, although he hoped that no one but Lemaitre had guessed that.

A policeman was just outside the house, another hovering behind the starched lace curtains of the front room. The policeman outside saluted and the man inside called something, and disappeared. A moment later, he opened the door. As he did so, Ruby Benson came hurrying from the kitchen, wiping her hands on a pink apron and then stretching behind her back to unfasten it. Something made her stop. The apron fell, crumpled, about her waist, and she stood squarely in the small passage, looking up at Gideon with the kind of defiance he had half expected.

"I don't want the children to hear what we say," she said; "they've had enough trouble already."

Gideon said, "All right, Mrs. Benson" in his mildest voice. "Where shall we go?"

She pointed to the front room, and followed him in.

The constable closed the door. Outside, there was Gideon's shiny car and more policemen and the curious neighbors—men, women and children. Outside, somewhere probably within easy reach of this house, was Syd Benson, the killer, the seeker of vengeance. His wife's face now held all the strain that it had shown years before, at the time of the trial.The youthfulness had faded. Even her hair seemed flat and lifeless, and the sparkle was gone from her eyes. It was a pathetic, almost a shocking sight.

Gideon knew her well enough to know that she was going to fight for what she wanted, no matter what he said: as she had fought before, to make the terrible decision to give evidence against her husband.

She said flatly, "You're not going to pester the life out of that boy."

Gideon held his felt hat loosely in both hands, in front of him. The woman didn't come much higher than his shoulder, and he probably weighed twice as much as she.

His head was only inches from the ceiling, so he dwarfed both her and the room.

"No," he agreed, "that's the last thing I want to do, Mrs. Benson, but I must talk to him."

"That's the same thing."

Gideon said, "I've talked to you. Have I pestered you?"

She didn't answer.

"Listen," Gideon said, "I've six children of my own. Six." He gave a little, wry grin, and she was so surprised that momentarily she relaxed. "Quite a handful. The eldest is twenty-six, the youngest a year or two younger than young Syd. I know children from the nappy stage upward. I know what they think like and what they feel like, and I know that if you start raising your voice at a boy like your son, and drive him into a corner, all you get is defiance and probably lies."

She didn't speak when he stopped.

"He ran away for one of two possible reasons," Gideon went on very steadily, "and the first is probably the right one. The television show upset him, and he was so riled at me and the fact that you seemed to be on my side, that he couldn't stand it any longer. Lots of children take a run like that—good Lord, I don't have to tell you! If that was it, then it's over. He's let off steam, and now he's come back under his own. You couldn't ask any more."

She asked, "What's the other possible reason?"

"He could have been to see his father."

Her face was suddenly twisted with alarm. "Oh, no!"

"Well, I don't think it's likely, either," said Gideon, "but we've got to find out, Mrs. Benson, and I think you and I are the people most likely to get at the facts. Think you can tell when he's lying?"

She didn't answer.

She didn't cry, "Yes, of course!" or attempt in any way to spring to the defense of her son. It was an odd thing, Gideon reflected gloomily, that she should be so absolutely honest, so naturally good. What had brought her to marry a man like Benson? The question was as fleeting as the thought.

"Sometimes I'm not sure," she said.

"Well, let's try."

"All right. Do you—" She hesitated, and then turned away without finishing what she was going to say. "We might as well get it over. I was just making some pastry for supper, he likes hot pastry." What a story that told! And so did her tense, anxious plea: "Go easy with him, won't you?"

"You know I will," said Gideon. "By the way, I called the hospital up just before I came. Mr. Small's eye will be saved, and the scarring shouldn't be too bad."

At the closed door, Ruby turned to face Gideon, and there was a different expression in her eyes.

"Listen," she said quietly, "if it hadn't been for that man Abbott, Art would have got it full in the face. I know, I saw it happen. So don't blame Abbott, see."

Gideon couldn't find a word to say.

All the hostility which young Syd had shown toward Gideon a few days before revealed itself again. The boy stood with his face to the kitchen window, so that Gideon could see every feature, every line. He was struck, as everyone must have been, by the likeness between father and son, even to the set of the jaw and the tightness of the lips; and the defiance. Gideon had the uneasiest of feelings: not only that whatever the boy said couldn't be relied on, but that something had happened within him. It might be something that he had experienced while he was in hiding; it might be simply the effect of the television show and what was happening to him now. And his hatred, his resentment, viciousness, because of his frustrated love for his father, might be centered on Gideon.

"I just went to Charlie's," he insisted flatly.

"Why?"

"Knew he'd let me stay."

"Been there before?"

"Done jobs for him."

"How did you get there?"

"Hid in a van."

"What van?"

"Builder's van," Syd almost sneered. "It was in the yard."

"Anyone know you were there?"

"Course not. It stopped down Mile End Road, and I got out and went to Charlie's."

"See anyone else there?"

"You try staying at Charlie's without seeing plenty."

"See your father?" Gideon asked, in the same flat voice.

There was a pause; just a startled moment of hesitation, when the expression in young Syd's face might have been taken two ways: that he had seen his father, or else that he was astounded at the possibility that anyone should have thought he had.

Then: "No!" he burst out. "Course not!"

"Syd," said Gideon very firmly, "that's a lie."

Young Syd said, "You cops, you can't tell a lie from the other thing. You took him away from me, and now you're hunting him like a dog, that's what you're doing. Don't you talk to me!"

"Syd, where did you see your father?"

Young Syd's eyes blazed, his lips quivered, his hands were clenched and raised.

"I didn't see him, think I don't know what you're trying to do? Trying to frame me, the same way as you framed him, that's what. You dirty rotten beast, don't you talk to me!"

"Think he has seen him?" Gideon asked Ruby Benson a few minutes later.

She didn't answer at once.

Her eyes were like glass, and the rims were so red that they looked painful. Gideon doubted whether she had had a good night's sleep since Benson had escaped; or would have one until he was caught. He could tell simply by looking at her that she had a splitting headache; the crisis of the past few minutes had made it far worse. She put a hand to her forehead and pressed, as if to relieve the pain, and then said:

"I don't know; that's God's truth, I don't know."

"Is there anyone who might be able to get the truth out of him?"

"If he doesn't want to tell you, wild horses wouldn't drag it out of him," Ruby said; "he's just like his father in that respect. Just like Syd."

The simple boy, Simon, sitting in a comfortable chair at the Divisional H.Q., with a cup of milk and some chocolate biscuits beside him, stared at Gideon without smiling; blankly. Chocolate smeared his lips—lips which were never really dry. His small eyes were pale and weak, and the puffy eyelids were scabby. He had hardly any eyelashes, just a few fair hairs. His fat, flabby face looked as if the flesh was unhealthy, as well as the poor mind.

With him was a short, gray-haired man wearing a brown Harris tweed suit with the cuffs and elbows patched with leather—a master from the special school where this boy went. The master had told the Divisional Superintendent, who in turn had told Gideon, that sometimes Simon could talk so that almost anyone could understand him, but that under any kind of pressure his precarious control of his mind deserted him, and he could do little more than make grunting sounds.

"How long do you think it will be before he'll talk intelligibly again?" Gideon asked, but he felt hopeless.

"There's no way of telling," said the schoolmaster. "I know what I'd do, but you can't possibly do it."

"What's that?"

"I'd let him go home, that's all. He lives with his mother, who's out charring mornings and afternoons, to keep the two going. If he were settled in familiar surroundings, and allowed to go to school again, I think he'd be all right in a day or two. Normal surroundings help him —like the company of normal children. That's why he and two or three other afflicted boys are allowed in the playground of the big school. They don't feel so lonely, then. If Simon is kept here, or anywhere unfamiliar—well, this mental blankness might go on for days or weeks. It's a kind of paralysis due to shock; in some ways he's much more sensitive than the average person."

The schoolmaster seemed to plead.

Gideon said reluctantly, "Well, the best we can possibly do is to have him looked after—can't let someone who's been tossing acid about run loose. He might do it again, might do anything."

"I know."

"Who'd be most likely to know where he got the stuff from?" Gideon asked.

"I don't know," said the schoolmaster. "He was at the special school this morning, so I should think that someone gave it to him when he was going out for lunch. He had sandwiches. I questioned all the school this afternoon, but no one seems to have noticed him talking to anyone; all we know is that he was down by the docks. He often is —he loves to see the ships go out and come in. No one stops him, it's remarkable how kindly people are to someone like him."

"I suppose so," said Gideon. "Well, we'll be guided by what the doctors say; the one thing you can be sure about is that he won't be ill-treated."

"Oh, I know that," said the schoolmaster. They turned and walked away from Si, who blinked after them, and then picked up his cup of milk with a limp hand; he spilt a little onto his trousers and dribbled some down his chin, but he didn't seem to notice. A police nurse, behind him, just sat and watched.

In the next room, Gideon asked the schoolmaster, "Do you know anything about young Syd Benson?"

"Oh, yes, I teach special subjects at his school, and I've taught him for several years."

"What's he like?"

The schoolmaster answered very slowly, "He's got a good mind, as sharp as anyone's at the school. If he likes a subject, he's way out in front. If he doesn't, he makes no effort at all."

"What's his general character like?"

"Tenacious."

"Honest?"

The schoolmaster said painfully, "That's a very difficult question to answer, Commander. What is honesty in a boy like that? What is loyalty? To his mother or his father? I don't know. If you mean, does he actually steal from his classmates—no. If you mean does he fight to get what he wants, and force weaker children to give in to him—yes. We've a dozen children at the school who have a father—

sometimes father and mother—who aren't strangers to prison. Some of their children are good, some pretty hopeless. The simple truth is that with such a background they acquire different standards of normal behavior—of right and wrong, if you like. No child will ever believe that something his mother or his father does habitually is wicked. The child just assumes that his father is right, and the rest of the world is wrong. That's how you get generation after generation of criminals. Commander—they're bred less by conditions than by the attitude of mind of their parents. As for young Syd—well, I didn't know him much before his father went to prison. I know he was sullen for twelve months afterward, and then seemed to start getting on top of himself. But it was a common thing to hear him talk about 'when my Dad comes out'—and could I, could any of the teaching staff, discourage him?"

Gideon said gruffly, "I know the problem."

"I'm sure you do," said the schoolmaster. "I only wish I could help you now. The woman I feel so sorry for is Mrs. Benson; now she has had a raw deal. The way she's brought those two children up—well, young Liz is a model example. Sometimes I think this talk of environment and the attitude of the parents is all poppycock, even though I dish it out myself! I begin to wonder whether some children are born with a kink, and others with a natural goodness. There couldn't be two more different children than the Bensons. How is Mrs. Benson?"

"Looking as if she'll crack up if we don't catch Benson soon," said Gideon, "but I think we will, Mr. Thomas. Thanks very much for all you've told me."

After Gideon had gone, after supper, during the evening, Ruby Benson sensed that her son's eyes were on her all the time, watching her, lynx-like, as if he wanted to know what she was going to do next.

And three times he asked her how her headache was.

She kept saying, "I've had worse," but that was hardly true. Soon, she would get the children to bed and then go herself, although she knew it would be impossible to sleep. When she lay down, she would have some more aspirins.

Unless her head got worse, when she would have them sooner.

20 . Night

By half past seven, it was pitch dark. Except in the main roads, the East End of London is not well lit.

Patches of bright lights glowing in the sky from the docks, where ships were being worked under arc lights, showed up clearly. The colored lights from cinemas showed up, too, red or blue, green or yellow, bright against the gray darkness of the sky.

It was a cloudy night.

In the little streets, so drab and mean, there was an uneasy quiet, a stillness which wasn't normal. Every now and again there was such a night as this, when the police of the Division had been reinforced by hundreds of men from outside, and the whole of the district was combed. The people knew why. Not more than one in a hundred had ever committed a felony or committed a crime of any kind—but one in five, perhaps even a greater proportion, knew someone who had: a friend, a relation, a husband, wife or daughter, brother or child.

The whole district knew the story of Benson and his wife, of Arthur Small, the missing boy and his return. None of them took Benson's part—except, perhaps, one or two like Charlie Mulliver, who knew which side their bread was buttered on. Benson's record had been widely known long before his trial; most people knew that he had been lucky not to be sentenced to death. The story of the murder of Taffy Jones in the car park had gone through the East End—as through much of the country—carrying with it a shiver of horror. Everyone knew, now, that Benson would kill rather than be taken, and there was a full realization among the people of the East End that he would almost certainly make an attempt to kill his wife.

The police came from other Divisions and from Scotland Yard, not in petty numbers but in their hundreds. They arrived by car, on bicycles, by bus, in Black Marias. They were watched, at certain focal points, by quiet crowds, and the temper of the district was best shown by the fact that there were few catcalls, little derision.

Under instructions from Divisional officers who knew the district inside out, the great search began.

There were private homes by the hundreds where Benson might be hiding, but Gideon and the Divisional people doubted if he were in such a place; someone was likely to squeal, someone would be glad of the few pounds blood money that he would earn. Benson wasn't likely to trust himself to any man unless he could rely on him absolutely—and those on whom he could rely, as far as Gideon knew, were being watched; that night, their homes would be searched first.

Quietly, the police went about their business.

As quietly, there was an exodus from the East End; not so big and not so noticeable, but quite as purposeful. For if this Division was being strengthened by reinforcements, then the neighboring Divisions were being correspondingly weakened, which made a heaven-sent opportunity for burglary. Every man who could force a window or open a door was on the move that night. Next day, the results of all this would show in the report placed before Gideon. And he knew exactly what was happening, but could do nothing about it.

If Benson was in London, he had to be caught tonight.

They searched Charlie Mulliver's place again; there was no result, nothing to suggest that Benson and Tisdale had been there.

They searched every room occupied by known friends of Benson; with no result.

They searched the docks; the warehouses; ships, small boats which were covered up in the backwaters; barges; lighters; dock installations; factories; empty houses and big warehouses away from the river.

They had a master plan of each part of the district, which spread over the whole of a great wall in the basement of G5 Headquarters; and here Gideon and the Divisional Superintendent, Simpson, with Chief Inspector Trabert who had been with them the previous night, watched quietly, saying little, seeing how the police were closing in. It wasn't the first such raid and it wouldn't be the last, but from each one the police learned something. This time, they had started on the perimeter of the district —the river on one side, and the main roads on the other, and went through it methodically. A second cordon was placed round this whole area on a wider radius—on the other side of the river, for instance, where anyone who sneaked across in an unlighted boat was bound to be noticed. But the river police were not patrolling openly; that was in the hope of luring Benson to the river if he was driven out of his hiding place.

No one could be sure whether Benson knew about the search or not; but even if he didn't know, he might guess.

As it happened, the old warehouse now used for temporary storage of petrol and other oils in drums was almost in the center of the area being searched, and the police were gradually closing in on it. As reports came in by telephone, radio and messengers, so flags of different colors were moved on the maps; and the precision of the raid was such that it looked like a continually narrowing circle.

Gideon was smoking his big pipe.

For once, this chase was the only job on his mind; obsessional. Deep down, he had the glum feeling that he might have made a mistake, that Benson might not be here. It was even possible that young Syd's disappearance and the attack on Small had been to fool him—Benson might be somewhere else, out on the outskirts of London perhaps, or at one of the ports, laughing his head off.

Only, Benson seldom laughed.

Three reports came in in quick succession from a Squad numbered, for the occasion, as South 21. They were coming up from the river, working their way through warehouses, and reporting each warehouse or large building that they had checked. Gideon, standing by the map, watched the Superintendent move a green flag from one warehouse to a line which showed another.

"That's near Rum Corner, isn't it?" he asked.

"Yes."

Gideon nodded, and drew at his pipe. Rum Corner was plumb in the center of the area being searched.

In London, not far away, Mary Rose was lying awake, tears stinging her eyes. Her brother lay asleep in the remand cell at Brixton Prison. Her mother lay, also asleep, in the next room. A mile or two away, Mrs. Edmundsun, so newly widowed, was looking at travel brochures, and every now and again at the scintillations from a pair of diamond earrings which had come to her only that afternoon. Detective-Sergeant Cummings, a bachelor who lived with a widowed mother, sat in his bedroom-cum-office at home, and smoked, and concentrated on everything he knew about Elliott, Edmundsun's manager. In another direction, Abbott lay, awake, feeling viciously angry with himself but a little easier in his mind now, because a message had come in—via Gideon, although he didn't know it—that Mrs. Benson had seen the attack, and had sent a message thanking him for helping to save her Arthur's sight. Arthur Small himself lay unconscious, under drugs, with a bandage round his head covering one eye. The two men who had broken into Kelly's Bank, earlier that week, were together in a room with some floorboards up, where a fortune in notes was hidden; they took some out and then replaced the floorboards—for the first time they were beginning to feel safe. Only half a mile away from them, Chief Inspector Lemaitre was looking at his blonde wife, and listening to her strident complaints. He was nearer revolt against her perpetual nagging than he had ever been; and one of the reasons for that was that he wanted to be on duty with Gideon.

In their different prisons, the other seven men who had escaped from Millways were sleeping; and the only one who would wake with a reasonably light heart was Matt Owens, who knew that when Gideon said he would make things easy, he would make them easy. At the Yard, the Information Room was a constant buzz of noise as reports of burglaries started to come in; Squad cars were hurtling round London, the Divisions were up to their eyes in work, and Sergeant Jefferson was quietly making notes, ready for the report that Gideon would want to see next morning. In his house, Superintendent Wrexall was very pleased with himself; for he was to go out to Guildford next day, about the accountant who had died an "accidental" death which might prove to be suicide. Wrexall had real cause for satisfaction, for one of the dead man's clerks had said that he thought that the accountant had been blackmailed; which proved that Wrexall's nose for blackmail was as good as ever. At Hurlingham, Kate Gideon was still up, and kept looking at the clock. It was a new, or at least a long absent feeling, to be worried about her husband; but after his narrow escape last night, she would be worried until they had caught Benson; and she knew how much the capture mattered to George.

The five Gideon children in the house were asleep.

Ruby Benson wasn't yet in bed, for the night held terrors for her. By the side of her bed, placed there with unexpected and touching solicitude by her son, were two white tablets. Soon, she would make herself take a milk drink, and take them.

Benson and Tisdale were awake.

Freddy Tisdale stood at the side of the window of the little office, looking sideways along the narrow alley toward a road which led to the docks. He had been there several times in the past hour, and when he wasn't standing there, Benson was. There had been no message of any kind for the past two hours; then, Charlie Mulliver had placed a lighted candle in the window opposite, a sign that the police had searched there and gone away.

In other words, all clear.

But it wasn't all clear.

Benson and Tisdale knew that, although they had not spoken of it. There were too many noises. Cars coming and going, men walking, the st-st-st-st-st of motorcycles which were being increasingly used by the police in London. It was possible to sense when the police were out in strength, and, without stepping outside the warehouse, these two knew it. Benson had seen one little group of police move in a body past the end of the street in one direction; Tisdale had seen another group at the other end of the street.

And they had heard men walking about in a warehouse adjacent to this.

Benson went out, suddenly, crept down the stairs, and reached the barrels of petrol. The screw cap of one filler hole was loose. He took it off, then rolled the barrel over until petrol spilled out, the smell almost choking him.

He went back to the office.

Tisdale moved away from the window, and spoke in a hoarse, spluttering whisper: "How do we know they're looking for us?"

"That's right," said Benson.

"Don't just sit there, what are we going to do?"

Benson said, "We're just going to sit here until they come. The streets are lousy with them, we wouldn't have a chance out there. When they start coming in, we go up to the roof. Then—"

"They'll search the roof!"

"Listen, Freddy," Benson said, "you wouldn't be losing your nerve, would you?" When Freddy Tisdale didn't answer, he went on: "If we run for it now we'll be seen, and we'll never get on board that ship. Now—"

"We ought to have gone earlier, we stayed too long."

Benson said coldly, "We stayed because I arranged it, and because the ship doesn't sail until the morning tide. We go aboard at the last minute, see, we don't hang around. One of the crew might recognize us, or there might be some river police taking a peek. They don't leave anything to chance, and you know it." In his harsh, clipped voice, Benson seemed to be talking sense; and to be steadying Freddy. "Now, listen. We go up to the roof. We jump across to the roof next door. It's a three-yard gap, and we could do it blindfolded. They've been there, haven't they?"

Freddy muttered, "Yes. But if they leave a man outside, watching . . ."

"And what if they don't?" asked Benson. "Can you tell me any way we can do it without taking risks?"

"If you hadn't seen your kid they might not have known we were in London, they—"

Benson moved, swiftly, savagely. Freddy gave a startled squeak of alarm. Benson gripped his wrist, so tightly that Freddy couldn't move his arm without risking a broken bone. In that moment they were at the level of beasts; and Benson was deadly.

"That kid didn't squeal, understand? If you say that kid squealed—"

"I didn't say it! I meant if we'd left here last night instead of tonight . . ."

"The cops can get a warrant to search a ship any time they like, or they can send the customs men on board," Benson growled. He still gripped Freddy's wrist hurtfully. "If we'd gone aboard, we'd be caught by now, every ship in the docks has been searched tonight. If you used your brains you'd know that. You going to listen to me?"

"Ye—es," Tisdale muttered.

"Okay." Benson let the man's arm fall. "If they come in here, we go up to the roof and jump. We wait until they leave here, and then we jump back. They'll know we've been here, and they'll search everywhere else, understand? They won't expect us back."

Freddy muttered, "We haven't got a chance, and you know it."

"We've got a chance if you keep your nerve," said Benson. "Okay, let's . . ."

Then they heard footsteps coming along the alley. They stood quite still. The footsteps were slow and deliberate, of policemen. They could tell that there were five or six men out there, walking in single file, going toward the main doors of the warehouse.

Freddy began to shiver.

Benson said, "Okay, Freddy, let's go," in a soft voice, and he took Freddy's arm and led the way toward the stairs. It wasn't the first time he had known a thing like this: some men were as brave as men could be when they were on the run, but once they were cornered, they lost their nerve. Like Freddy. In these past few minutes, Benson had realized that Freddy's nerve was cracking, and that he would be a passenger from now on.

Benson couldn't afford a passenger.

But he did nothing yet.

They went slowly, stealthily, up the wooden stairs. They heard muffled sounds below. They opened the hatch which led to the roof, and looked about them. They saw the gaunt outline of the roof of the adjoining warehouse, shown up clearly by the glow from the docks, where a ship was taking on the last of its cargo before closing the hatches and setting off across the Atlantic for Buenos Aires.

No policemen were on the roof.

Benson said, "You go first." They had studied the spot, and knew exactly what to do. There were a few yards to spare, so that they could get in a short run before they leaped. Freddy, his teeth chattering now, made ready to run. Benson watched him, quite coldly, knowing exactly what he was going to do. Once on the other side, he would use his knife to silence Freddy.

He also had a gun, which Charlie had obtained for him; if he were cornered, he would use the seven bullets in it for the police.

He knew, deep down, that he had always intended to go away alone.

But he didn't want Freddy's body found on this roof; better leave it on the other, which had already been searched.

Freddy started to run. Benson could hear his hissing breath, knew that he was really frightened, his nerve quite gone. There was one good thing, he couldn't miss the opposite roof—anyone could clear ten feet even from a standing start.

He saw Freddy falter, at the last split second.

He realized that Freddy just hadn't the nerve to jump, and that was all about it.

He rushed forward, but he was seconds too late. On the roof of the other warehouse, two policemen had suddenly appeared. Freddy had seen them first, and Benson had been so busy watching him that he hadn't noticed. Now they were clambering toward the edge, and suddenly a whistle shrilled out in warning to the police below.

And Freddy Tisdale, trying to check himself, was so close to the edge that he slipped.

He screamed as he crashed down.

Benson swung round, as the scream rose to the night sky.

The glow of light showed the roofs of the warehouses clearly, and revealed policemen springing up on several of them, men who had stayed on the roofs of the warehouses which had been searched, so as to watch the street and to give warning.

Benson's only chance was to go down the stairs. It wasn't really a chance, probably no one else would have tried to take it. But he ran, drawing the gun from his pocket as he went.

In the room at the Divisional H.Q. Gideon saw the glitter in the eyes of a radio operator who was receiving a message from a Squad outside, and heard the shrillness of his voice:

"Tisdale's fallen off a roof! Benson's at the old Subra Warehouse."

"Come on," said Gideon.

Ruby Benson was standing in front of the gas stove, in a dressing gown which Art Small had given her, small feet in heel-less slippers. She was watching the milk as it heated. The two white tablets hadn't been touched.

21 . Last Throw

Benson reached the landing of the second floor of the warehouse as the police reached it from below. There were three of them, and he had a split second's advantage, because he was sidling close to the wall and they were rushing up, two men level with each other and the third just behind. Others were below. Whistles were shrilling, men shouting, someone fell over an empty barrel and the booming sound echoed clearly.

Benson jumped forward.

He fired three times, and scored two hits, wounding the same startled policeman in the leg and the waist. This man lost his balance and fell against the others, and as they were pushed to one side Benson leaped past them. He reached the half-landing, turned, and fired again as one of the men picked himself up and prepared to leap down the stairs. He didn't know whether he had scored a hit, but the man stopped. He went rushing toward the ground floor, and another policeman, clearly visible in the lights which were flashing from side to side, blocked his path. The man saw the gun and, without hesitation, flung himself to safety. Benson passed him, and then reached the big storage room, near the barrel which he'd partly emptied earlier, the reek of petrol still in his nostrils. He struck a match, and flung it at the pool of petrol.

The match went out.

Benson saw it go out, and knew that he hadn't a chance even of the vengeance he had wanted. So he stood close to the wall, watching the men who were momentarily wary of him, able to see those on the ground floor and anyone coming down the stairs. He slid his right hand into his pocket and took out a matchbox, opened the matchbox with one hand, then put it to his lips and tossed three tablets into his mouth. They were like the tablets he had sent to his wife.

That was the moment when the policeman who had lost his nerve found it again and leaped at the killer. He judged the moment to perfection and clutched Benson round the legs, clawing him down. The tablets spilled from Benson's lips, the gun went off and a bullet wasted itself.

Next moment, the cold steel handcuffs were on those sinewy wrists.

Gideon entered the warehouse about five minutes later, and already a lot had been done. Emergency lights had been rigged up from a car battery, the big ground floor was lit, not brightly but enough for everyone to be seen. A dozen uniformed and three plain-clothes police were standing about, and there was a stir as Gideon came in, with Trabert and Simpson close behind him; Simpson was a tall, bony man, and in this light he looked almost skeleton thin.

Benson was handcuffed to a burly detective-sergeant, and standing as erect as a man could be, feet firmly planted, shoulders back, eyes narrowed but glittering, mouth set tightly.

He didn't speak as Gideon came up.

Gideon said, "This was the way it had to end, Benson; why the hell didn't you have some sense?" His voice sounded tired; he wasn't tired, but fighting against showing his hatred for this man, determined to appear impartial instead of bitterly hostile. He paused, and looked at the killer for what seemed a long time, watched intently by all the rest. Then: "What did you say to your son this morning?"

He saw Benson start, and then begin to look incredulous.

Gideon went on: "The kid's young. If he goes on the way you've started him, he'll end up on the same place. Give him a break, Benson. What did you say to him?"

Benson said in a grating voice, "Did the kid squeal?"

It would have been so easy to say yes; to make him suffer this awful disappointment; to send him on his slow, laborious journey to the gallows with a new hate in his heart. Gideon knew all that, and could not bring himself to do it.

"No," he said, "he didn't squeal, but I happen to know children. What did you say to him?"

Benson didn't answer.

The light in his eyes was radiant.

Only a few hundred yards away, in the house in Muskett Street, Ruby Benson put the tablets into her mouth, and then sipped the hot milk.

When it was obvious that Benson wouldn't talk, and that Gideon had nothing more to say, the sergeant in charge started talking: How Benson had tried to take the tablets, two of which they had salvaged, one of which had been trodden under foot. How one wounded man was on the way to hospital, but not likely to be on the danger list. How a constable had defied Benson's gun, and collared him. All this, while Gideon looked about him, nodded at the policeman who had brought Benson down, in a way that he was likely to remember all his life, and looked at the tablets.

"Trying to kill himself, was he?" he asked. "What's in them, Benson?"

Benson's eyes still held that glow; that new, precious pride in the son who had not failed him. It was a form of exaltation. Gideon realized it, and felt a kind of nausea because it could come to this man and in this way.

"Come on, what's in them?" Gideon demanded.

Then Benson made his one mistake.

"Why don't you ask my wife?" he sneered.

Ruby Benson had been in bed for ten minutes, and was feeling a little queasy, when she heard the tires screech outside the house. She started up, staring toward the passage. A policeman was on duty in the front room, and she heard the door open, and heard his heavy footsteps. Next moment, a man strode in from the street, and spoke in a voice which she would never forget: Gideon's.

"Where's Mrs. Benson?"

"She—she's upstairs, sir, just gone to bed, she . . ."

Gideon didn't respond, except to start pounding along the passage and toward the stairs. Ruby clutched her silk nightdress tightly at the neck, and sat there, bewildered, feeling her heart race with heavy, throbbing beats. Gideon's footsteps thundered, the house shook, Liz and young Syd would be bound to wake.

Her door burst open.

Gideon drew up, at sight of her, gasping for breath. Then, more steadily, he moved toward her, and answered the question that was in her eyes.

"Yes, we've got him, it's all right. Did young Syd give you any tablets tonight? Aspirins, or . . ."

She raised her hands in sharp, stabbing alarm; and in that moment she told Gideon "yes" without having to utter the word. She saw the panic in his eyes as he went on urgently:

"Where are they?"

"They were aspirins! I've just taken—"

Gideon swung around toward the policeman behind him.

"Get some salt, mustard, make a strong emetic—and get a move on!" Now, his voice was controlled and calm, although it was obvious that he imposed the self-control with great difficulty. He was so big, so frightening, so full of menace. "It's all right," he told Ruby, "you'll bring them up and they won't do you any harm. Just a few unpleasant minutes. Benson gave them to young Syd—"

"Oh, no," she cried, "no, not young Syd, no!"

Gideon walked into his office, at ten o'clock next morning, and found Lemaitre and the Assistant Commissioner, Jefferson, Wrexall and two other superintendents all waiting for him. The morning report looked thick enough for a week instead of a day; Lemaitre had spread himself.

Gideon grinned round, for a welcome like this could lift him out of depression, help him to forget the wounding of the evil things he fought.

Question and answer took twenty minutes until gradually the men left the office; and finally only Lemaitre, Gideon and the A.C. were there.

"There are about thirty newspapermen after you," the A.C. said, "I told them you'd hold a Press Conference!"

Gideon shrugged.

"Why don't we just give them a list of men on the Force? Then we'd all get some limelight." He loosened his collar as he unbuttoned the desk, but he didn't sit down.

"Benson won't say a word, of course; I don't think we'll get anything out of him now or later. Thank God his wife's all right, though."

"You say the tablets contained one of the opiates?"

"Yes, Mulliver says he got them from a ship's captain who sailed out yesterday morning. He'll be held when he reaches port. Mulliver supplied Benson with the gun, too. Still, Mrs. Benson's been lucky. She'll get over it all, of course; but she'll be a sight happier if we could prove that young Syd didn't know what was in them."

"Think he did?" asked the A.C. quietly.

"I don't know," said Gideon, "I just don't know. I don't want to think that he did, the thought that a kid of twelve would give his own mother—well, we'll have to work on him, that's all. Through the family doctor or his school teachers, or—" Gideon broke off, and shrugged. "Main thing is that Arthur Small will definitely be all right except for a scar which won't be too prominent."

"Good," said the A.C. "Good."

He went out, soon afterward; and Lemaitre, who was usually very subdued during the great man's presence, relaxed at once and jumped up. He squashed out a cigarette and started to take out another.

"Wish to hell I'd been able to get there, but you know what it's like with Fifi." Gideon not only knew what it was like, but realized that they must have patched up their latest quarrel, for Lemaitre showed none of the sourness that was too often in his voice when he talked of his wife.

"Well, we can sit back and take it easy, now the whole bunch is caught."

Gideon looked at the report.

"Who's been kidding you?" he asked dryly.

"Oh, that's only routine," said Lemaitre. "Every man

who can force a door must have been busy last night, but there was no big stuff taken. They picked up Jim Ree again, had his rope ladder ready at a place in Grosvenor Square. It's all there in the report, anyway. Three of those notes from the Kelly's Bank job turned up this morning from a restaurant in Soho; better get over there pretty quick, might be able to find out who passed them. Arkwright says will you spare him ten minutes, he wants to check a couple of points on the case coming up at the Old Bailey on Monday. Cummings has found out that Mrs. Edmundson's been getting a lot of travel literature, and Elliott bought a pair of diamond earrings recently. Cummings is a sticker; if we ever pin anything on Elliott, we'll have to thank Cummings. Well, that's about the lot, and it's all there—oh, no, it isn't!"

"What else?" Gideon asked evenly.

"Smedd rang just before you came in, said would you ring him back. Wants to rub your nose in it, I expect."

"Hmm," said Gideon. "Maybe." He put the call in, and didn't have to wait long. He was already in as good a mood as he was ever likely to be in, because when he had got home last night he had realized just how edgy Kate had been about him; and just how deep was the new affection between them. So much was good.

But a girl who was lying bravely to save her brother . . .

"Good morning, Commander," said Smedd, in his hard, brisk voice. "I thought you would like to know of two new pieces of evidence in regard to the murder of Winifred Norton, and the charge against William Rose. A regular cinema goer who attended the Roxy Cinema last Thursday for the performance which Rose's sister states she and her brother also attended, has made a statement. This statement declares that Mary Rose was with a young man, whose description might possibly tally with that of her brother. Also, a clerk in the same office as Rose has stated that three days before the murder he had tried to borrow Rose's penknife, but Rose told him he had lost it. Further inquiries about the evening of the murder have brought to light the information that an older man was seen with the murdered girl near the spot where her body was found. This man has not yet been identified, but I am of course making the closest possible inquiries. . . ."

As he listened, Gideon's eyes grew very bright and his hopes ran high.

THE END